DANGER COMES CALLING

Elaine Driscoe and her sister Kate expect their walking holiday along Offa's Dyke Path to be a peaceful pursuit — until a chance encounter with a mysterious stranger casts a shadow of fear over everything. Their steps are constantly crossed by three men — Niall, Steve and Phil. But which of them can they trust? And what is the ultimate danger that awaits them in Prestatyn?

KAREN ABBOTT

DANGER COMES CALLING

Complete and Unabridged

LINFORD
Leicester

First published in Great Britain in 2004

First Linford Edition
published 2005

British Library CIP Data

Abbott, Karen
    Danger comes calling.—Large print ed.—
Linford romance library
    1. Love stories
    2. Large type books
    I. Title
    823.9′14 [F]

    ISBN 1–84617–028–1

Published by
F. A. Thorpe (Publishing)
Anstey, Leicestershire

Set by Words & Graphics Ltd.
Anstey, Leicestershire
Printed and bound in Great Britain by
T. J. International Ltd., Padstow, Cornwall

This book is printed on acid-free paper

1

Niall Foster heard the text message alert on his mobile phone and pulled his open-topped Porsche into the first lay-by he came to. The message was brief and to the point.

Target M Cardiff rlwy café 15:00

He glanced at his watch. It was 13:51. He had plenty of time. He put his phone back on to the seat beside him, checked that the road behind him was clear, flicked the indicator switch and swung back smoothly on to the road.

The wind blew through his fair hair, exhilarating his senses. His brilliant blue eyes sparkled with the thrill of the chase as his lips curved in a sensual smile of satisfied anticipation of the success of his assignment. The familiar buzz of adrenalin was already coursing through his lean body, as it always did when he was on a case.

Just over an hour later, Elaine Driscoe alighted from the Liverpool to Cardiff train and carefully lowered her bulging rucksack to the ground. Tucking her long, fair hair behind her ears in a well-practised gesture, she looked about her.

'Where is she?' Elaine wondered out loud.

Kate's train had been due in ages ago and she didn't want them to miss their connection to Chepstow. Her face creased into an anxious frown. Her nineteen-year-old sister was not particularly well known for her punctuality.

Elaine stooped down to pick up her rucksack by one of its shoulder straps and swung it over her right shoulder. A signpost part way along the platform indicated that refreshments were available. She had suggested to Kate that they meet in or near the café, and so she headed towards it.

The cafeteria was crowded. Elaine searched the faces and shapes of the backs of other heads but it was clear that Kate wasn't there.

Well, there was no point in going anywhere else to look for her. They could end up chasing each other round the station. Oh, well! She might as well have a cup of coffee while she waited.

Carefully carrying a tray with her coffee and a sandwich on it, she sought a place to sit. Very few seats were free and she needed to get two for when Kate arrived. A table in the far corner had only a man and a young woman sitting at it. The woman seemed to be of Malaysian origin and the man European. They probably wouldn't mind sharing. From the look of it, they were having an intense conversation. The man had a camera in his hand and was obviously explaining something about it.

'Excuse me. Do you mind if I sit here?' Elaine asked, nodding her head towards the two empty seats.

'What?' The man broke off abruptly. 'Oh! No, I'd rather . . . that is, please yourself! I'm going now!'

He rose to his feet, knocking into the table, causing the young woman's barely-touched coffee to spill over the top of the mug. He made no apology.

'Remember what I said!' he said sharply to the girl, nodding his head in emphasis to his words, then without waiting for a reply, he began to thread his way between the tables towards the door.

As Elaine lowered her tray to the table she saw that the man had left his camera.

'Is it yours?' she asked the girl.

The girl looked at her with frightened eyes.

'No!'

Elaine picked it up and ran after the man.

'Excuse me! You've left your camera!' she called.

He looked over his shoulder and spread his hands.

'It's not mine! She said it doesn't work. I was just looking at it.'

Elaine was taken aback. His eyes were devoid of warmth and she felt a shiver run down her back. She hesitated and looked back to where the girl was sitting, an extremely worried expression on her face. When Elaine turned round again, the man had gone.

A fair-haired man at the next table half-rose from his seat, as if he were about to leave but when Elaine began to return to her table, he sank back on to his seat again.

Sparing him no more than a cursory glance, other than to register his extremely attractive face, Elaine shrugged her shoulders as she retraced her steps.

'He said it's yours,' she said, placing it on the table.

The girl seemed so agitated that Elaine wished there were spare seats somewhere else. But there weren't.

The girl dropped her eyes.

'I'm sorry. I not speak good English. I not understand.'

'That's all right,' Elaine said casually. She seated herself opposite the girl, which gave her a good view of the door and window, enabling her to keep a look out for her sister.

'Please?' the girl asked.

Elaine smiled, waving her hand in an apologetic way.

'It doesn't matter.' She touched the camera. 'Is there a problem? Shall I look at it? I'm quite good with cameras and it looks the same as mine.'

She tried to make her meaning clear with gestures.

Her eyes wide with alarm, the girl snatched the camera from the table and hugged it to her chest.

'No! No!'

She began to make hasty movements to gather her bag and camera.

The girl thrust the camera into her bag and half-stood up, still looking extremely agitated.

'Please, don't go,' Elaine begged. 'It's my fault. I'm sorry I've disturbed you. Look, I'll move somewhere else.'

She glanced around, but the only empty seat was a single on the next table. The fair-haired man raised his eyes from his newspaper but he made no welcoming gesture. Elaine felt a stirring of interest in him. He was good-looking and something about him made her wish she had met him somewhere different.

'Elaine!'

Elaine turned in the direction of the voice. It was her sister.

'Kate!'

Her cry of pleasure was greeted by a wide smile from Kate, her face lighting up as she vigorously pushed her way between the tables. Her dark auburn hair seemed to leap around her head as she shrugged her rucksack out of the way of people's heads.

'My train got in early so I went to look around,' Kate said in explanation, hugging Elaine.

'It's great to see you, Kate! Sit down! I'll get you something to eat. Will a sandwich and coffee be all right?' She looked at her watch. 'We've got plenty of time.'

'Yes, fine. Tuna mayonnaise, if possible.' Kate sat down next to the Malaysian girl. She smiled at her in her usual friendly way. 'Hi!'

A flicker of a smile briefly lit the Malaysian girl's face but she made no audible reply. Elaine returned with another tray of sandwiches and a mug of coffee for Kate.

'How were your end-of-term exams?' she asked. 'Did you get through all right?'

Kate pulled a wry face.

'Yes, but only just. I need to get down to it next year. They're more strict with second years.' Her face brightened. 'But I needn't think of that right now. It's holiday time and, boy, am I in need of it!'

'Me, too!' Elaine smiled.

She had just completed her first year of teaching and welcomed the summer break as much as Kate.

'Tell me a bit more about where we're going,' Kate demanded. 'I'm sorry I had to leave all the arrangements to you but what with swotting

8

and exams and . . . everything . . . ' A tiny smile hovered on her lips but she didn't say why.

Elaine knew her sister well.

'Not forgetting fun, fun, fun!' Elaine teased.

She undid the top zipped pocket of her rucksack and pulled out two books, four printed sheets and two clear plastic bags. She handed two of the printed sheets to Kate.

'Put one of these in the plastic bag and the other in a zipped pocket of your rucksack as a spare. It's a list of all the places we'll be staying at, with the addresses, phone numbers and ordnance survey grid references. I've given a list to Mrs Harrison, as well, since she's keeping a neighbourly eye on our house while we're away.'

'Bolton's Private Agent for Protection of Property!' Kate joked. However, she looked impressed. 'You've been busy!'

Elaine smiled dismissively.

'I enjoyed it. It's given me an insight

into some of the lovely areas we'll be passing through.'

She handed over one of the books next.

'These are our guide books, complete with maps and written directions. Each book covers half of Offa's Dyke Path. I've marked off each day's journey, where we leave the path, and an arrow leading to the approximate position of our bed and breakfast.'

'Elaine Driscoe! Did you ever consider training officers for commando exercises?' Kate asked, laughter dancing in her eyes. 'Have you marked our rest places with an asterisk?'

'What rest places?' Elaine countered, keeping her face straight.

Kate shot her a startled look but was relieved to see that Elaine was teasing her.

'You had me worried there, for a minute,' she confessed. 'But, go on. Tell me in words of a few syllables where we're going and how far we travel each day.'

'Right! Well, we get the connection to Chepstow in, let me see . . . ' She glanced at her watch again. ' . . . in half an hour. We'll find our B&B and then go out to Sedbury cliff to do the first couple of miles of the Offa's Dyke Path back to Chepstow. The guide books recommend doing that in the evening if you're staying overnight in Chepstow, so that you can set off the following day in a northerly direction. Then, sister, dear, we can enjoy ourselves looking around the town and maybe the castle, have a meal somewhere, then early to bed! Tomorrow we start out in earnest, about twelve to fourteen miles a day right up to Prestatyn on Sunday, August eleventh, two weeks tomorrow . . . almost two hundred miles away!'

Kate's wow of awe was obliterated as the young woman next to her jumped visibly and knocked her cup of coffee across the table. She leaped to her feet, her face flaming with embarrassment.

'Don't worry!' Elaine tried to soothe her, pulling a wad of tissues out of her pocket and mopping at the spreading liquid.

The girl's olive skin flamed red.

'I sorry! I sorry!' she stammered.

The café's manageress came over with a cloth in her hand.

'Don't worry! I'll clean it up. D'you want another?'

'No! No! I must go! Thank you! You so kind!'

She grabbed her handbag and, pushing past Kate who had also risen to her feet, she rushed out of the café without a backward glance.

'Poor girl! She was quite upset,' Elaine commented, her eyes following the girl's fleeing figure.

As she re-seated herself, she became aware that the man at the next table was looking at her intently as he rose to his feet. After the merest hesitation, he also left the café.

Two hours later, they had forgotten about the incident. They were in Chepstow town centre, merging with holidaymakers thronging the main street. Overhead bunting added a carnival atmosphere and the girls temporarily forgot their forthcoming long-distance walk. A group of acrobats and tumblers announced an historical re-enactment attraction being held in the castle grounds. Checking their list, they asked for directions to Bridge Street and eventually found their B&B after searching up and down the street, making no sense of the numbering system that followed no chronological order and kept starting again at number one!

They dumped most of their baggage, keeping only a small day-sack, camera, guide book and bottles of water and set out for the coast. They went through a wooded area, following a well-worn track and it wasn't long before they could see the River Severn and the elegant, curved bridge that spanned it.

A low, stone monument marked the official start of the path. A walker who had just completed the walk in a southerly direction obligingly took their photograph and they took his with his camera.

Later, after a welcome shower and change of clothing, Elaine and Kate once more joined the tourists who were enjoying their summer holiday in the town. They had afternoon tea in a very nice café and gradually their footsteps led to the outer walls of the castle that dominated the small town.

The group who specialised in re-enactment of various historical periods was enthralling the crowds with a portrayal of mediaeval life. Elaine and Kate gladly paid their entrance fee and sauntered into the castle grounds, immediately transported back through the ages.

A trumpet fanfare heralded the approach of a mediaeval knight on horseback. The sheer size of the horse sent a thrill of awe through the girls as he cantered by. Then a rat-catcher displaying the proofs of her skill called out, offering her services. Farther on, an archery competition was in full swing.

'Let's join a guided tour,' Elaine suggested. 'We only have a limited amount of time, so we can't see everything.'

They did so and were soon being told of historical events and long-ago folk-lore of the town's rise and fall in history's timeline.

'And over here, ladies and gentle-men, is the Great Hall. Over at the far end, on the raised dais, the lord and his knights would sit in splendour at the high table . . . '

Elaine's attention wandered momen-tarily as the guide's voice droned on telling of the splendour of yesteryear.

In the far corner, through a large, open serving-hatch, there seemed to be an argument going on. A young woman pulled away from what seemed to be a man's hand.

'No! No!' her voice carried across the space.

Elaine touched Kate's arm.

'I wonder what's going on over there.'

'Hmm? What's that?' Kate turned round to see where Elaine was pointing but she couldn't see anything unusual.

'There was a girl. She sounded frightened.'

Curious, Elaine took a step towards the scene.

Kate restrained her.

'Don't be a nosey parker! Listen to the guide. It's interesting.'

Reluctantly, Elaine followed the group as they moved on through a broken, stone archway and down a flight of steps to the ancient cellar.

The group of tourists obediently stood still as they listened to the explanation of how the provisions for the castle came up the river and under the castle walls where they were unloaded, to be carried by a string of servants up to the storerooms.

Elaine's attention wandered. She suddenly realised that the group had turned and were now coming back towards her, retracing their steps to where a flight of stone steps led upwards, within the castle wall, to the upper floor.

Finding herself now at the front of the group, she led the way to the foot of the staircase.

A flurry of movement to her left caught her attention. A young woman hurtled round the corner, looking frantically over her shoulder. Whatever it was she saw, it caused her to draw her breath in sharply. As she turned back, her eyes had the look of a hunted stag — bright and fast-moving, looking for a way of escape. If the party of tourists turned to go up the steps in front of her, her path of escape from whoever was following her would be cut off.

It was the white dress as much as her face that made Elaine suddenly recognise her. It was the Malaysian girl whom they had sat next to in the café earlier that day. Instinctively, she paused, halting the rest of the group.

The girl flashed her a brief glance. Was it of gratitude, or a plea for help? Everything happened so fast, it was

17

impossible to tell. The look of fear changed into swift recognition and then hope. As she sped past the group, the girl thrust her hand out towards Elaine.

'You go to Prestatyn, yes? Take this, please! I see you tonight at the festival! If not, I see you at Prestatyn.' She made as if to go but hesitated and turned back. 'Do not use camera. It not . . . '

She obviously couldn't think of the right word.

' . . . work?' Elaine suggested, remembering the scene in the café.

'Yes. Thank you!'

With that, the girl rushed up the stairs and disappeared around the corner.

Elaine glanced down at the camera in her hands. Was it the same one the girl had had in the café? It looked like it.

The pressure of the group pushed Elaine forward in the wake of the fleeing girl. Looking back over her shoulders as she mounted the first two steps, Elaine could see a tall, fair-haired young man, his suntanned face impatiently straining from side to side as he tried to push his way through the group. As their eyes met, she gasped. It was the man from the café . . . the second man, the one who had left after the girl.

Was the girl fleeing from him? Elaine couldn't be sure, but he definitely wasn't part of their group. Elaine knew she would have noticed him earlier if he had been.

His expression showed his impatience at being held up but he had no option but to wait. It was a narrow passageway and the flow of the group carried them forward, blocking his way. By the time the last of the group had reached the top of the stairway, the Malaysian girl had disappeared.

As soon as they had left the castle grounds, Elaine told Kate what had happened, watching her sister's eyes widen in wonder.

'Are you winding me up?' Kate asked, finding the tale hard to take in.

'What do you make of it?'

Elaine shook her head.

'I really don't know. It does seem incredible, doesn't it?'

She took the camera out of her day sack and looked at it. It looked very ordinary, certainly not an expensive one. Why had the girl given it to her? Did it hold an incriminating photograph of someone or something important?

The girl probably wished by now that she had kept it, since she had got away from her pursuer. And, to be honest, Elaine wished the same thing herself. This holiday was to get away from pressure, not to take it with her.

'So, does that mean we go to the show tonight?' Kate asked.

It was advertised as a spectacular show of light and sound, telling the story of William Marshall, a landless knight who had risen to be one of the most powerful men of his time. Music, laser lights and fireworks were promised, plus a cast of over one hundred actors.

Elaine nodded, although she had earlier advised against it since it only began at ten o'clock and they really needed an early night.

'Yes, we'll have to. I won't feel easy until I've given this back to her.'

Having decided that they weren't suitably dressed for visiting a restaurant, they bought fish and chips from a local shop and ate them out of the paper wrappings, sitting on the bridge over the River Wye overlooking the castle and its grounds across the river.

Elaine would be relieved when the camera incident was over with.

Not wanting to be conspicuous by being back inside the castle grounds too early, they waited until they had seen a fair number of people re-entering the grounds before they joined them.

'Where shall we sit?' Kate asked.

'I don't want to be trapped in the middle.' Elaine mused. 'Let's sit here on this wall. We'll be able to see the stage and, hopefully, the Malaysian girl will see us and come to claim her camera.'

The summer sky was darkening when the music began and laser lights began to dance around the battlements or shoot up into the sky, displaying hologram pictures of ghosts of people of long ago whose lives had played a part in the long-gone drama. Large speakers were positioned all around the battlements and voices began to tell the tale in speech and song. It was breathtaking in its imagery and, for a while, Elaine forgot their real purpose in being there. The music, singing and dancing lights worked in harmony, creating an enchanting fantasy.

Suddenly, a search beam picked out a slight figure dressed in white. The movements were agitated and Elaine found herself staring intently at the figure. Was it the girl she hoped to meet? At this distance, she couldn't tell. The light began to move on, picking up the next group of actors now leaping jubilantly along the battlements. As it did so, a dark figure seemed to loom up against the girl.

The bright beam retraced its path and hovered for a moment . . . but the battlements were deserted.

2

A burst of fireworks illuminated the sky, accompanied by a crash of music. Tumultuous applause greeted each fresh burst of silver, gold or other shining, coloured stars. Sound and light erupted from all sides of the building and a host of holograms danced and whirled.

Elaine heard none of it. Her eyes were fixed on the empty battlement. Where was the girl? Had she fallen? Had she been pushed?

She couldn't be sure. As more fireworks lit the sky amidst more hologram pictures against the night sky, she wasn't even sure any more if she had seen anything at all.

Gasps of, 'Ooh!' and 'Ah!' leaped from numerous lips as yet more fireworks spread their glittering cargo into the night sky.

Maybe she had imagined it.

'Wake up, Elaine!'

It was Kate, shaking her arm. She was laughing.

'You were well away! It was great, wasn't it? I'm glad we came! Aren't you?'

Elaine struggled to concentrate. She couldn't dismiss her fears lightly.

'Y . . . yes, it was. Only . . . '

She felt shaken but didn't know what to say. She hadn't actually seen the girl fall. She had simply vanished from sight.

Elaine tried to shake away her heavy forebodings. Surely the Malaysian girl would appear at any minute to claim the camera and she would hand it over and that would be that.

Only the girl didn't come.

They waited until most of the people had left the castle grounds and it was only when officials began to give them enquiring glances that they decided that they could do no more by waiting any longer for the girl. The only course of action was for them to leave the castle grounds and return to their B&B.

As they made their way through the still busy streets, Elaine told Kate what she had seen . . . thought she had seen, she corrected herself.

Kate wasn't over impressed.

'It was probably a trick of the lighting,' she suggested. 'There was so much happening all at once, you probably mixed up the various scenes in your mind.' She playfully dug her elbow into Elaine's ribs. 'You are getting on, you know!'

'Cheeky! I'm not yet twenty-three!'

'Sounds old to me!'

'Just you wait! Your time will come!'

'Anyway, you never know, we might see her tomorrow.'

Elaine sighed.

'Maybe. She said she would see us in Prestatyn if she didn't see us tonight.'

'Well, there you are then! She knows that's where we're heading. She'll find a way to contact us there in two weeks time. Forget about it for two weeks!

We're on holiday!'

Kate made it sound easy and Elaine made an effort to do as she suggested . . . but, inside, she was uneasy about the whole thing. She couldn't help looking repeatedly over her shoulder as they returned to the guest house where they were staying overnight. A hot shower helped to relax her and she soon fell into a restless sleep.

The following day dawned brightly and, after a good breakfast, the girls were on their way shortly after nine o'clock, their rucksacks neatly packed and carried high on their shoulders.

The first part of the route was through woodland along a slippery path and by the time they emerged into the open again, rain was falling.

With a groan, the girls lowered their rucksacks to the ground and pulled out their waterproofs. This was not going to be a glamorous holiday! As they passed a huge, flat rock, known locally as the Devil's Pulpit, they paused to look down upon Tintern Abbey, 'way below in the valley.

'It says here that the devil used to stand on this rock and preach blasphemy to the monks, to corrupt them,' Elaine read out from the guide book through its plastic cover.

Kate laughed.

'I can just imagine him dancing on the rock in fury when the monks ignored him. Abbeys were pretty rich places without any help from the devil, weren't they?'

'Yes. Apparently, this was one of the wealthiest in Wales. Shall we go down and spend an hour or so there? We have the time.'

The abbey seemed even grander down at valley-level. The Cistercian monks had chosen the site well. It was surrounded by hills and woodland on three sides and banked by the river Wye on the fourth.

As they wandered around, listening through headphones to the recorded historical tour, Elaine could feel some of the tension in her involvement with the Malaysian girl was melting away. She stood in the centre of the nave, her eyes closed as she listened to the choral chanting, imagining the white-robed monks at worship in the Gothic-style edifice, envying the peacefulness of their ordered lives.

The sun came out again, streaming in through the ornamental stone tracery of the main window. Elaine pulled her camera out of its case and took a number of photographs, wanting to capture this special moment. Other tourists were there, some of them obvious walkers like themselves, taking a break off the official path. They exchanged a few words of jocular nature, knowing that within a few days they would be greeting them as old friends.

'How about a cuppa?' Elaine suggested. 'Once we're back on track there's nowhere else marked until we get to The Fish and Game at Redbrook.'

Kate agreed and offered to claim a table. They took off their rucksacks, automatically rolling their shoulders backwards and straightening their backs in relief at the lightened load.

When Elaine returned with the two mugs of coffee and slices of carrot cake balanced precariously on a small plate on top of each mug, a young dark-haired man was seated at the table with Kate, both in animated conversation.

'Hi, Elaine! This is Phil,' Kate introduced the man. 'He's a student, like me. He's doing the walk, too. Isn't that great!'

Phil nodded towards Elaine, his cheerful face beaming.

'Hi! We were just comparing notes. I'm pushing on to Monmouth today but we might catch sight of each other later on. I've not booked in anywhere beyond tonight, so I can be pretty flexible. Where are you aiming for next?'

Elaine wasn't sure she wanted to

make any commitments to meet up with anyone, nor to reveal too much of their planned itinerary, not while she still had the Malaysian girl's camera in her rucksack.

'I doubt we'll be going at your pace,' she tried to say lightly, not wanting to cause unnecessary offence.

Kate flung her a surprised look.

'It might be fun to meet up sometime,' she objected. She turned back to Phil and smiled. 'Take no notice of Big Sister. She forgets I'm grown up now. Well, I shall keep a good look-out for you, Phil.' She raised her mug of coffee towards him. 'See you on the road!'

Elaine felt exasperated by Kate's flippant attitude.

'Drink your coffee, Kate,' she said sharply. 'We need to be pushing on as soon as possible. It looks like rain again.'

'Yeah! Well, I'd best be pushing on myself,' Phil agreed, standing up and shrugging his rucksack on to his tall frame. He nodded towards Elaine's camera that was hanging around her neck. 'Want me to take a snap of both of you before I go?'

Elaine instinctively clutched the neck-cord tightly.

'No, thanks! We've already had one.'

'Suit yourself! See you on the road, ladies!'

With a parting wave of his hand, Phil strode off towards the exit-gate.

'Did you have to be so unfriendly, Elaine?' Kate demanded, once Phil was out of hearing. 'I felt so embarrassed!'

'We know nothing about him,' Elaine responded. 'He could be anybody! I just didn't want to give him my camera, nor for you to tell him our nightly stops. What if he's trailed us from Chepstow and wants to get the other camera back? Maybe he thought this was it!'

'Well, we'll never know. At least he didn't grab the camera and run off with it! Anyway, we don't know that anyone except the Malaysian girl wants the camera back,' Kate said reasonably. 'As for him trailing us, anyone on the walk will either be trailing us or us them! Are you going to get paranoid about everyone who overtakes us or offers to take our photograph together?'

Elaine grimaced in a self-deprecating way.

'Probably! I guess it's bothering me more than you because I saw the girl up on the battlements and don't know what happened to her.'

'Thought you saw, you mean,' Kate came back at her swiftly. 'I hope you're not going to let it spoil our holiday because if you are, we may as well call it off right now and get the train back home.'

Elaine appreciated the sense behind Kate's words. It was a strange position to be in, as she was usually the one with the commonsense and Kate the unpredictable one.

'I'm sorry. You're right, of course! I'm letting it get to me.'

She drank the remains of her coffee and stood up abruptly.

'Come on. I'll race you to the top!'

Neither of them took that challenge seriously but it restored their good humour and spurred them on their way. It was a fairly stiff climb back up on to the dyke and both girls were thankful when they reached there. From there, they walked on top of the dyke for some miles, admiring the views.

A few times they passed other walkers and, occasionally, individuals striding out on their own overtook them. Apart from brief acknowledgements, no-one made any other conversation and Elaine found herself able to relax about it.

By mid-afternoon, the rain started again and they hastily donned their waterproofs once more. At least they gave them an anonymity that Elaine welcomed, though with the rain pelting down and soaking them through, their concentration was more on each step they took, since they were now descending a steep, slippery slope that would bring them into the village where they were to spend the night.

A fortunate glance to the left as they stepped through a gateway on to the public footpath alongside the main road in Redbrook identified the name of their chosen hostelry, The Fish And Game.

A hot shower and a cup of tea soon revived them and they decided to completely empty out their rucksacks to make sure that the heavy rain hadn't found a way in to their clothes. When Elaine unpacked the Malaysian girl's camera she rocked back on to her heels, looking intently at the camera in her hands.

'It's just an ordinary camera. In fact, it's almost identical to mine, so I can't think that it's worth much in itself. It must be something to do with the film.'

'You mean like someone committing a crime . . . or something?'

'It's a possibility, isn't it?'

'Mmm. But why give it to you?'

'Perhaps the person chasing her wanted to get it off her to destroy the evidence. She recognised me from the café and must have decided she could trust me to take care of it for her.'

'We could put it in for developing if we pass one of those one-hour developing and printing shops. It might be safer to keep the photographs than the camera.'

Elaine considered for a moment and then shook her head.

'I'd feel I was invading her privacy.' She laughed nervously. 'I think I'd rather not know what's on the film!'

'Well, we could hand it in at a police station. I'm sure it wouldn't take us far off route to find one.'

It was a sensible suggestion and Elaine was tempted to go for it. It would take the responsibility off her shoulders. However, she had to acknowledge a reluctance to take that step.

'Possibly. I don't know, though. The girl entrusted it to my care. Her eyes seemed to plead with me for understanding.' With a determined move, she opened her rucksack again and thrust the camera deep into its inner bag. 'I'll keep it well-hidden for now and hope the girl finds us somewhere.'

★ ★ ★

Monmouth was the target for elevenses on Monday. After the loneliness of the hills, the town seemed to seethe with people. Pedestrians overflowed on to the roads in places, making car drivers short-tempered and given to making unnecessary tootings on their horns.

'I want to get some postage stamps,' Kate remembered suddenly. 'I've bought three postcards to send to college friends.'

'OK! I fancy a browse in this second-hand book shop,' Elaine readily agreed. 'Look, there's a café over there called Marlene's. Let's meet there for coffee in about twenty minutes.'

Elaine spent five minutes or so looking along the book shelves and eventually chose a book by one of her favourite authors. She pushed it into a side pocket of her rucksack and emerged once more on to the busy pavement. Kate was nowhere in sight and, with a hasty glance up and down the road, Elaine took a step forward off the pavement.

She heard a male voice say, 'No!'

In the same instant, a vice-like grip took hold of her upper arm and she was pulled backwards on to the pavement. She lost her balance and took a stumbling step sideways, but the firm grip prevented her from falling.

'I've got you!' a male voice spoke quickly.

Shaken by the words as much as by being pulled back on to the pavement, Elaine steadied herself and raised her head, and her eyes immediately widened in shock.

It was the man who had been seated at the next table in the station café at Cardiff railway station, the one who had risen from his seat and followed the Malaysian girl out of the café when she rushed away. He was also the man who had been following the girl in Chepstow Castle.

She saw his face in recall, remembering how she had looked back over the heads of the guided tour group. Her throat felt paralysed. If he was indeed that man, and she was sure that he was, why was he here, holding her in this manner? Had he seen what the girl had given her? Was he going to demand the camera off her?

His intense blue eyes held hers, though she was also aware of his sensual mouth, firm chin and fair hair. She felt a recurrence of her initial pang of instant attraction to him but it immediately was countered by a stab of fear.

'W . . . what do you want?' Elaine stammered, when she could force her vocal chords to function.

'Nothing,' he replied, an element of surprise in his voice.

Her heart pounded. Because you think I have something you want, she thought desperately, her heart hammering within her chest. You think I know something — except she didn't. Everything was a complete mystery to her.

How had she become involved in all this?

She tried to pull her arm free.

'You're hurting me!'

'Surely that's better than being killed under a car.'

His voice was deep and resonant. Normally she would have found it attractive but the way he had suddenly grabbed hold of her had unnerved her and she could only hear threat in his voice.

Her heart seemed to stop beating.

'Are you threatening me?'

'No. Should I be threatening you?' he asked, conveying a mixture of amusement and supercilious menace.

Elaine could feel her hackles rising. Who did he think he was?

'I'm not afraid of you!' she declared defiantly, watching his face.

'Aren't you?'

His lips twisted . . . in amusement, she felt.

A surge of anger began to rise within her.

'No.'

'Haven't we met somewhere? You seem . . . '

'No. I don't think so,' Elaine replied quickly, not wanting to be forced into admitting that she had recognised him. 'May I have my arm back?' she asked. 'I need to rejoin my sister. She's waiting for me.'

'I hope she looks after you better than you look after yourself!'

He released her arm but stood quite still, regarding her as one would look at a naughty child.

Elaine could feel herself withering under his gaze.

Kate's voice, calling, 'Elaine! Over here!' gave her the impetus she needed.

'Keep away from me!' she warned.

She looked quickly up and down the road to make sure the road was clear and thankfully made her escape across the road.

'Wow! Who was that?' Kate asked.

'He just grabbed hold of me!' Elaine told her, her voice stammering a little as the effects of the incident took hold of her.

Kate didn't look too impressed.

'I think I'd try to throw myself under a car if I thought someone like that would rescue me!' she declared.

'What do you mean? That's the man whom I saw in the castle on Sunday, the man who was chasing the Malaysian girl. And he was also in the café in the railway station at Cardiff.'

'What! Are you sure?'

'Positively.' She felt shaky.

'Well, he certainly saved you from a sticky end just now!' Kate declared.

'What do you mean?'

'He pulled you back just in time! Didn't you realise! You nearly stepped out in front of a car.'

Elaine stopped dead. Her hands flew to her hot cheeks.

'Are you sure? I thought . . . Oh, gosh, no wonder he looked at me like he did, like I was a spoiled child, or something. Oh, dear!' Had she just made a fool of herself? Yet, he was the same man! She was sure, or almost.

She turned around to see if she could still see him, but he had disappeared from sight.

3

The drink of coffee gave Elaine time to recover from the fright she had had but her mind was in turmoil as they trudged out of town through an old, stone gatehouse. Why did he have this effect on her? Or was she so jumpy that any good-looking man whose eyes held a certain magic would have the same effect on her?

She was glad when they left the town behind them and returned once more to the isolation of the countryside. The sun came out again and the steady rhythm of their steps through fields of waist-high corn or meadows containing grazing, long-horned cattle soothed the raw edges of her mind.

They spent that night in a modernised farmhouse about a mile off the path not far from a village called Llantilio Crossenny. Their hostess cooked a superb meal for them and, after a comfortable night's sleep, sent them on their way the following day, well-fed.

'We'll be getting fat, at this rate,' Elaine grumbled light-heartedly, fastening the waist-belt of her rucksack.

'Not likely! Not with the pace you set!' Kate laughed.

Although the rain held off, the air became decidedly cooler as they reached the top of Hatterall Ridge and they put extra clothing on before they began the exhilarating walk along the top of the ridge. At times, they felt as though the wind could have blown them away but they put their heads down into it and plodded on.

Both were thankful that they weren't completing the twelve-mile ridge-walk that day and they welcomed the sight of Llanthony Priory nestling down the enchanting Vale of Ewyas.

It was a pleasant surprise on reaching valley level and searching for their hotel for the night to discover that Abbey

Hotel was exactly what it said it was — part of the twelfth-century abbey itself.

The hotel part of the abbey was in the west wing of the Augustinian Priory and an original Norman spiral staircase led up to the room that the girls were to share that night.

They discovered that the dining-room, consisting of three vaulted bays, was formerly the prior's parlour. Elaine could imagine him eating his succulent meals at one of the antiquated tables. Farther on, at a lower level in what was formerly a cellar, they found the bar and gladly ordered two wedges of sinful-looking chocolate cake and two large glasses of orange juice.

'I'll take your photograph, Elaine, or people will wonder who came on this walk with me,' Kate joked. 'Say cheese!'

'A bit difficult with a huge wedge of cake between my teeth!' Elaine rejoined with a laugh, licking some cream off her fingers.

'Hi, you two! You've caught up with

me, then!' a male voice exclaimed.

Kate was already grinning a welcome and Elaine swung around to see Phil approaching their table with an equally-large wedge of coffee-and-walnut cake on his plate.

'Another unrepentant sinner!' Kate exclaimed, licking the last of the cream off her fingers. 'I wonder if the coffee cake is as scrumptious as the chocolate version.'

'Hands off!' Phil warned. 'This is mine!'

'Aha! This is how you get to know who your friends are!' Kate teased, reaching over with her cake fork.

A mock battle for possession of the plate followed, ending with Phil allowing Kate a tiny forkful of the desired treat.

'For testing purposes only!' he warned, ready to drag his plate out of reach.

'I shall leave you two children to fight it out on your own!' Elaine declared playfully. 'I want to look inside that lovely old church over there.'

Elaine left them to it, hoping she had got through to Kate about not divulging much information about their daily programmes.

The plain interior of the church lived up to her expectations and she was enthralled to read some of its history, how the second son of William the Conqueror, sickened by the useless, idle life at court, found the place whilst out hunting and found solace there, and in later years, under the sanction of Anselm, Archbishop of Canterbury, he was joined by like-minded men and they began a twenty-year building programme on the priory buildings.

'Lovely, isn't it?' Kate's voice spoke close by. 'And look, it's still in regular use today!'

Elaine smiled a greeting.

'I'll buy a couple of these postcards but I'd like a photograph of the outside. Did you bring my camera with you? I think I left it with you, didn't I?'

'Oh, gosh, you did! I didn't think

about it!' Kate apologised. 'Hang on, I'll dash back for it!'

Elaine followed her and was in time to see Kate stop abruptly part way across the lawn. She could see at a glance that the table-top was bare. Her camera had gone!

A young lad in a red and blue checked shirt and faded denim jeans was pushing his way through a group of tourists who looked as though they were part of a coach tour making their way back to the carpark. The lad seemed anxious to get away from the area.

'Hey!' Elaine called after him, beginning to follow him through the crowd.

The tourists were mainly elderly people who were none too steady on their feet. They glared at Elaine as she tried to weave her way amongst them.

'I'm sorry! Excuse me!' she apologised over and over. 'My camera has been stolen! Someone has taken it! A lad! Over there!'

The lad was no longer in sight.

Elaine stood on tiptoe, trying to see above the heads of the people near to her but without success. There was no sign of him, and she didn't know for certain that he was the thief.

She went as far as the corner of the building but there were then too many directions he could have taken, either back into the abbey somewhere or over a fence into fields or on to the road. Feeling annoyed with both herself and Kate for leaving the camera, she stood with her hands on her hips, looking in each direction in turn.

It wasn't an expensive camera but it was adequate for the purpose and she enjoyed taking snaps of such events in her life. Their parents, at present on a cruise among the Greek Islands, would be disappointed also to have no record of their holiday to pore over.

'Elaine! What are you doing?' Kate was calling her, anxiously threading her way towards her. 'Did you see someone take the camera?'

'I'm not sure. There was a lad making

off in what seemed a hurried way. I don't know if he was the thief, though.'

'I'm sorry. I really didn't realise you had left it. It's generally hanging round your neck,' Kate apologised.

'Yes. Well, you were the last one to use it. I just hadn't picked it up again.'

'Sorry!' Kate apologised again. 'Are you going to report the theft?'

Elaine grimaced in annoyance.

'I suppose I'd better, just in case it turns up. The thief might realise it's only a cheap one and discard it, mightn't he?'

Elaine made her way to the reception desk in the bar to lodge her complaint. It hadn't been handed in and Elaine left their room number, just in case it was handed in later. She then rejoined Kate outside again.

'I'm not blaming you, Kate,' she apologised. 'I'm as much annoyed with myself for not picking it up when I went off to see the church. What about Phil? Did he leave before you or afterwards? Could he have taken it?'

'Elaine! You're not still suspecting everyone who speaks to us, are you? He left at about the same time as I came to find you and I assure you . . . '

'No! I was only thinking he might have realised it was mine and be trying to find us.'

They were out in the open again, unintentionally approaching the car-park. Elaine raised her head and looked around, wondering if Phil was still around. Suddenly, she caught sight of a youth wearing a red and blue check shirt. She grabbed Kate's arm.

'That's him! That's the lad I saw running off through the crowd.'

The youth was talking to a man sitting in the driving seat of an open-topped, dark green car. She saw him hand something dark to the man and receive a piece of paper in return. Was it money?

'Hey! You there!' she shouted. 'Come here! I want to speak with you!'

She began to run in his direction.

The youth jerked up his head and

stared at her for an instant, before taking to his heels and running swiftly between the cars, over the fence and back into the crowds outside the abbey.

Elaine knew it was pointless to follow him.

She turned towards the car, only to hear the engine spring into life. At a speed that was dangerous in such a confined space, the driver reversed out of the parking bay, threw his gears into first and second with barely a pause and it, too, shot out of the carpark and away up the road.

In the fleeting glimpse that Elaine had of the back of his head, she fancied that his hair was fair, though, in all honesty, she couldn't say definitely that it was the same fair-haired man who seemed to be dogging their steps.

'Well, what do you think of that?' she demanded of Kate as her sister joined her.

'What happened?' Kate asked, looking mystified about her behaviour.

'I told you! It was the lad who

pinched my camera. At least, I think it was. He was selling it to the man in that car. Now what would a grown man with an expensive car like that want with a cheap, automatic camera that he could buy for less than twenty pounds anywhere?'

'Are you sure? It happened very quickly.' Kate shrugged her shoulders. 'At least it wasn't Phil,' she couldn't help saying. 'This rather clears him, doesn't it?'

'I suppose so. Sorry I've been so suspicious about him. I don't feel I can trust anybody at the moment.'

'What is it with you and cameras?' Kate asked rhetorically. 'You're given one you don't want, and the one you own gets stolen. You'd better buy yourself one of those single-use cameras, hadn't you? Otherwise you'll be a right grouch for the rest of our holiday. In fact, why don't you use the Malaysian girl's camera until we meet up with her? It's the same model as yours. You could take her film out and keep it safe to give her when we give her the camera.'

Elaine stared at her.

'Kate, I think you have just hit the right nail on the head.'

'What d'you mean?' Her eyes widened as Elaine's meaning sank in.

'Oh, I see,' she breathed slowly. 'You think the thief thought he was stealing the other camera. But how did he know you have it?'

'I don't know for sure, but the man in the car could have been the man we bumped into in Monmouth. It looked a bit like him. He could have pointed me out to the lad, or described what we look like.'

Surprisingly, the thought gave her no satisfaction. She felt as though she was betraying him, yet she hardly knew him, did she? He could be anyone.

'It's a possibility, isn't it?' she added reluctantly, glancing nervously about them. 'Whoever he is, he must suspect that the Malaysian girl has given us the camera and maybe he overheard us in the café at Cardiff saying that we are walking Offa's Dyke Path. No-one's been obviously following us today, have they? At least, I don't think so. We would have seen him up on the ridge. I think he's taken a chance that we would stop here sooner or later. Most people do, with it being so near to the path. Anyway, the man's gone now. He thinks he's got what he wanted.'

She felt saddened somehow by her conclusions. She didn't want the fair-haired stranger to be the one who was pursuing the Malaysian girl.

Kate still looked a bit sceptical.

'It could be sheer coincidence. If it was that lad you saw, he might have just seen it on the table and nicked it whilst he had the chance.'

Elaine frowned. 'But why try to sell it on so quickly? Why didn't he get as far away as he could? No, I think it was planned. The man must have hired him beforehand, promising to pay on delivery. The thing is, what will he do when he discovers it's not the right camera? He can't know for certain that I have the one he wants, not unless the Malaysian girl has told him so. And, if that's the case, why didn't she come herself? She knows I'll hand it over to her straight away.'

'He'll probably think he's made a mistake and leave us alone,' Kate suggested hopefully.

'Or he'll come back and try again,' Elaine countered. After a pause, she laughed briefly. 'I bet we're making a great big mountain out of a tiny molehill. We've read too many spy stories and thrillers. Let's get back inside,' she suggested to Kate. 'Even if the man tries to contact us again, he can't possibly know we're staying here tonight.'

'Do you think you'll recognise the man if you see him again?'

Elaine looked worried. 'I only saw a glimpse of him, but if it's the man from Monmouth and Cardiff, I'll know him.'

His face was somehow indelibly imprinted in her memory.

With a show of light-heartedness that she didn't feel, Elaine linked her arm through Kate's, but she couldn't help mulling over in her mind that the glimpse she had had of the man in the car did look like the man who had accosted her in Monmouth.

★ ★ ★

At that same moment, Niall Foster was driving his Porsche swiftly back towards Monmouth. The usual exhilaration after a successful snatch had been made was missing. Instead, he was filled with a sadness he couldn't explain.

It was strange, he reflected, recalling the coincidental meetings he had had with Elaine, if they were coincidences, that was. His eyes narrowed as the memory of a line from Goldfinger, of James Bond fame, came to mind. What was it the man had said? 'Once is happenstance, twice coincidence, three times enemy action.' Is that what Elaine was? An enemy?

His train of thought side-stepped for a moment and he mused upon her name for a few moments, repeating it softly in his mind before snapping back to the present.

Was she part of the opposition?

Unaccountably, he hoped not. Even though he didn't really know her, he couldn't bear to think of her getting hurt . . . and things could turn out nasty in this business.

Who was she? It was funny, but even that first time of seeing her in the railway station café, it was as if . . . as if he recognised her, he decided. He gave a short laugh. He wasn't usually best known for being of a fanciful nature. Down-to-earth, you-get-what-you-see type of bloke was more his line . . . except when he was on an assignment, of course. Then, he could act and evade like the rest of them.

He pursed his lips thoughtfully as he shook his head in bewilderment. What was it about this young woman that moved him so?

He didn't know.

All he did know was that their meeting had happened at the wrong time and the wrong place . . . and he couldn't help wishing that the timing had been different.

4

As Elaine and Kate walked along the northern part of Hatterrall Ridge the following day, they could see the dark mountain range on their left, realising why the Black Mountains were given their name. They had a forbidding majesty about them and, for the present, Elaine was thankful that they were only crossing the fringe of them. She had enough foreboding of her own to entertain her mind!

Three hours later brought them to the end of the ridge. It was a bleak, stony area. A trig point indicated that it was the highest point of the Offa's Dyke Path.

'Let's stop and have a snack,' Elaine suggested. 'It's a lot warmer now we're off the ridge, and look, there's someone coming down behind us. He's moving a lot faster than us. This will be a good spot to let him past us.'

Inwardly nervous of whom it might be, she was relieved to note a friendly expression on the young man's face when he quickly drew level with them. They smiled a brief acknowledgement to him, although Elaine in particular wasn't anxious to strike up a conversation, however harmless he appeared.

The man, however, looked intently at them.

'Excuse me, but didn't I see you at Llanthony Abbey yesterday?'

'M . . . maybe,' Elaine replied cautiously.

'Probably,' Kate agreed simultaneously. He was quite dishy, she thought admiringly. 'We were there. Did you enjoy your visit?'

'Yes. It's a lovely place, isn't it?'

He paused, then added hesitantly, 'Did you . . . er . . . lose anything?'

'Why, yes!' Kate agreed quickly, aware that Elaine would preferably have snubbed his advances. 'A boy stole Elaine's camera.'

'I thought so! I didn't actually see him do it, but I suspected as much. He was trying to sell it to people. I saw one man refuse it, then he offered it to me for ten pounds. I hope you don't mind. I took the liberty of taking it off him. I thought I might see you again.'

He took his rucksack off his back and rummaged in it.

'Here it is.'

Elaine felt wary, trying to recapture the scene of the theft, but Kate squealed with delight.

'Oh, you angel! Isn't that wonderful, Elaine? You've got your camera back again!'

'Y . . . yes.' Elaine accepted the camera from his extended hand. 'Thank you.' She began to open her waist-bag to get some money out but the man laid a restraining hand on hers.

'No, I didn't give him any money. I told him I'd seen him pinch it. He was off like a shot, I can tell you!'

Elaine fingered the camera. Something was niggling at the back of her mind but she couldn't quite grasp hold of what it was.

The man noticed her preoccupation.

'I'm afraid the back has been opened. Your photographs to date have been lost and you'll need a new film. Were the photographs important?'

'Only as part of our holiday.'

'We can always start again and take some more,' Kate joked.

'Are you doing the whole length of Offa's Dyke Path?'

Before Kate could answer, Elaine said quickly, 'We're walking where it takes our fancy. You know, here today and somewhere else tomorrow.'

Kate looked surprised.

'Thank you again for my camera,' Elaine said dismissively. She hung it around her neck again, glad that the other was out of sight in her rucksack. 'It was very kind of you.'

'Not at all,' the young man rejoined pleasantly. 'My name's Steve Martin, by the way. I may see you again. I'm walking along Offa's Dyke myself.' He smiled at Elaine and held out his hand. 'I gather you are called Elaine, and your friend?'

Kate giggled. 'We're not friends, we're sisters . . . and I'm Kate.'

Steve took her hand and bowed over it in an elaborate way.

'I must hope to bump into you again. Are you going far today?'

'Only as far as Hay-on-Wye,' Kate replied before Elaine could stop her.

'No! What a coincidence! I'm staying there myself. We'll probably meet again later on. I'll look out for you.'

He waved his hand in a farewell salute and continued his descent of the ridge.

'Honestly, Elaine, you really are the limit!' Kate exploded as soon as he was out of earshot. 'What is the matter with you? Surely you don't think he had anything to do with stealing your camera. He's the one who's brought it back, for heaven's sake.'

'Yes, I know, but something doesn't quite add up,' Elaine said slowly. She

65

had just remembered what it was that niggled her. 'I know I saw the man in the car take the camera at the abbey. He certainly didn't refuse it. So how did Steve get hold of it?'

'Well, you must have been mistaken,' Kate exclaimed impatiently. 'Why should he lie about it and then give it back to you? Honestly, Elaine, you're reading far too much into this. I've a good mind to make you throw the other camera in a rubbish bin as soon as we see one.'

'Maybe the other man realised that it was the wrong one and has got Steve to return it, hoping to befriend us,' Elaine mused, unable to shake off her unease. 'I don't know. I just wish you hadn't told him where we're staying tonight.'

'What was the point in lying? He's going our way, anyway, so he might see us there,' Kate pouted. 'Besides, I like him. It'll be fun bumping into him every so often. You said that's one of the appealing things about long-distance walking. People you meet one day are greeted like old friends a few days later.'

'Mmm, maybe. I don't know. And I didn't mean you should have lied to him. Just try to be a bit vague and say something like, 'We'll see how far we get.' At least you didn't tell him the name of the guest house.' She made herself smile to lighten the mood. 'Just don't go getting too involved with him, Kate or with anyone else.'

'Like Phil, you mean?' Kate's voice was decidedly cool.

'Like anyone! We know absolutely nothing about anyone we might meet and I feel very uneasy about the whole thing. This could be some serious business. Until we decide what to do about it, I don't feel we can trust anyone at the moment.'

'I'm beginning to think this whole idea of us being on holiday together was a mistake from the start,' Kate exclaimed. 'It's no wonder you've no steady boyfriend. You probably frighten them all away, or freeze them out.'

'I've had plenty of boyfriends, thank you very much!' Elaine snapped. 'And I don't freeze them out. It was me who finished with Marcus, don't forget, not the other way round.'

'Only because you found out he was two-timing you!'

'And the rest. Anyway, I'm just wary of picking up any strangers, the way things are.'

They slithered and slid carefully down the lower end of the ridge, mostly in silence but once they were striding out again, their good humour returned. Pleasant fields and pastures lay ahead of them as they approached the Wye Valley and it was mid afternoon when the town of Hay-On-Wye suddenly came into view. It was a busy, thriving town, known nationally and internationally for its numerous bookshops.

Tourists abounded and, finding that the Seven Stars Hotel was not yet open for admission, Elaine and Kate joined the throng meandering through the streets. The appetising aroma of home-made bread attracted them to The Granary, a shop and café selling traditional home cooking.

'Mmm! My mouth is watering,' Kate admitted as she sniffed the air appreciatively, shrugging her rucksack off her back. 'Grab a table and I'll get us something gooey to eat and a drink.'

Elaine sank on to a chair and unfastened the laces of her boots, easing her feet out of them and wriggling her toes.

'Ah, that feels good!' she couldn't help saying as she leaned back in her seat. 'Oh, sorry.'

She had accidentally leaned into someone. She swivelled round on the chair and found herself looking up into a pair of smiling blue eyes. It was him again — the fair-haired man of previous acquaintance. She jumped in alarm and almost fell off her chair as it skidded backwards.

'You again!' she gasped before she could stop herself.

The man put out a hand to steady her.

'Hello! We do seem to keep bumping into each other, don't we? And no offence taken! In fact I can identify with your relief.' He placed his tray on the table and pointed down at his own boots. 'I'll be glad to do the same thing.' He indicated one of the vacant seats. 'May I? Only if I'm not intruding, that is.'

'Yes! I mean, no. That is . . . my sister will be joining me.'

She was shaking. An instinctive part of her wanted to get to know this man, sensing that he would be important to her . . . a soul mate. The other part warned her to be wary of him. Whatever her natural attraction was to him, she intuitively knew he meant trouble . . . and, possibly, danger.

The man smiled disarmingly, causing tiny laughter lines to crinkle at the edges of his eyes.

Elaine's heart did a series of acrobatics. She tried to quench them but without success.

The man wasn't put off by her lack of enthusiasm for his company.

'That's all right. I can cope with two young ladies at once.' He leaned towards her confidentially. 'Tell me, are you always this nervous?'

Elaine glowered at him.

'I'm not nervous! Why should I be?' she denied swiftly. Her expression darkened. 'What are you doing here? Why are you following us?'

'Strangely enough, I was about to ask you the same question. Chepstow, Monmouth and now Hay-on-Wye.'

Elaine blushed. She had denied remembering him from Chepstow. He obviously hadn't believed her.

'We're walking Offa's Dyke Path,' she protested indignantly, forgetting her instructions to Kate about keeping that fact to themselves.

'Ah!' The man smiled innocently. 'That must be it. So am I.'

'I don't believe you.'

He spread his hands.

'It's a free country. Walking is one of my passions.'

'And what are the others, besides stalking people and making yourself a nuisance?'

He held up his hands in mock surrender.

'Ah, I'm accused of that all the time,' he agreed. 'I'm in management,' he added. 'Allow me to introduce myself. Niall Foster from York. And you are?'

'Kate and Elaine Driscoe from Bolton,' Kate's voice supplied over Elaine's head, nodding her head down at Elaine as she spoke her name.

Niall smiled, rising from his seat to take the tray out of Kate's hands and placing it next to his on the table.

'I see we have similar tastes.'

He indicated the huge wedges of cherry almond cake that sat on the three plates, each with a swirl of thick cream decorating the top.

He dug his fork into his wedge of cake and placed a sizeable portion into his mouth.

Elaine's eyes felt drawn to his mouth as his lips closed over the cake.

Elaine seethed. She felt she should either have insisted that he moved to another table, or that she should have picked up their own tray and moved elsewhere themselves but, apart from the fact that the outside seating area was filled to capacity, there was some magnetism about the man that prevented her from moving.

His tanned face was ruggedly handsome and the laughter lines at the outer corners of his eyes seemed to be a permanent fixture, as if he smiled a lot. A dimple at the lower end of his left cheek deepened and, amazingly, she felt that she wanted to reach out and touch it.

'And are you walking by yourself?' Kate asked, drawing his attention to herself. If Elaine was determined to freeze him out, it didn't mean that she had to do the same, although he was a bit on the old side for her, really, going on thirty, she reckoned. Still, he was tall, lithe and super-fit and quite made Phil and Steve seem rather juvenile in comparison.

'Yes, and no,' Niall answered enigmatically. 'I'm with a group from my work-place, you know, one of those bonding assignments we managers are keen on these days,' he added, as Elaine's right eyebrow rose in sheer disbelief.

He beamed at them both, but his eyes lingered on Elaine.

'And what do you do for a living, Elaine? Let me guess.'

He scrutinised her face, bringing a blush to her cheeks.

'Someone who likes to be in control, I guess and thinks men can be a pain at times.' He laughed at the outraged expression on her face. 'I'm right, aren't I?'

'No . . . you . . . are . . . not!' Elaine said in stilted, staccato words.

'Yes, he is!' Kate contradicted.

Elaine kicked her shin under the table and glowered warningly at her.

'I happen to be a teacher,' she said primly. 'Not that it's any business of yours, Mr Foster.' She emphasised his formal title and surname.

Niall only laughed.

'Niall. I insist. We're already on first-name terms. I refuse to take a backward step after making your acquaintance. Besides, all those in my group call me Niall. They wouldn't know whom you were meaning if you used my formal title.'

'I hardly think that matters, since we're not in your group and not likely to meet again,' Elaine said coolly. She picked up her fork and delicately broke off a small section of cake and placed it in her mouth.

'Oh, I don't know,' Niall demurred. 'We were trailing you from Hay's Bluff this afternoon and I'd say you go about the same pace as we do. And, since I'm acting as sweeper, I think we might be seeing quite a lot of each other. Don't you, Kate?' He turned to smile captivatingly at Kate again.

She grinned back at him, deciding that, in spite of Elaine's unease about him, she liked him.

Niall had poured his tea whilst talking and now drained his cup. As he stood to make his departure, his glance fell upon the camera around Elaine's neck.

'Would you like me to take a photograph of you two girls?'

He held out his hand in expectation of being given the camera. Elaine recoiled back from him.

'No!'

The word came out more explosively than Elaine intended and her cheeks reddened.

'There's no film in it,' she added lamely. 'I need to get one.'

'Ah. Then, maybe some other time?' he suggested. 'I expect we'll see you later. Until then, bye-bye.'

Elaine felt her heart was torn as he left them. Strangely, it was beating in a most irregular fashion, and it wasn't because of her fear that he might be involved in the mystery surrounding the Malaysian girl's camera.

'And what are you grinning about?' she asked Kate.

Kate puckered her brow as if deep in thought.

'Now, what was it you said about not talking to strangers?' she asked sweetly.

5

The Seven Stars was open when Elaine and Kate returned. They registered their names and followed Mr Williams, the proprietor, out of the rear door and up some steps to a well-appointed room over the small swimming pool that belonged to the hotel. It was one of the only two swimming pools in the accommodation booklet that Elaine had used and they had both considered the extra weight of a swimsuit each in their rucksack was worth it for the pleasure of a swim.

'It was lucky you had booked the accommodation,' Mr Williams commented, as he unlocked the door. 'I could have let my rooms three times over today.'

'Really?' Elaine was instantly alert. 'Whom did you turn away?'

'A couple of small groups of young men.'

Elaine felt herself relax in relief. No-one could have followed them here, then. That was good.

It was a pleasant room, with two single beds and an en-suite bathroom. If they undressed and showered quickly, they would have time for an hour's swim before having to go out to find somewhere for their evening meal.

It was heavenly to dive into the unrippled pool and feel the cool water on their bodies. Whilst Kate performed a few dives at the deep end, Elaine swam half a dozen lengths in stylish front crawl and then flipped over on to her back to repeat the sequence. She had completed a turn at the shallow end when she was aware of a splash behind her.

Her mind registered that it was a loud splash for someone of Kate's slender build but made nothing of it. It was only when a gleaming male body surfaced at her side and Niall's laughing eyes twinkled down at her that she realised her mistake.

'What are you doing here?' she spluttered, her body inelegantly losing its poise and sinking beneath the water.

She struggled to regain balance and found Niall's hand cupped under her left elbow, steadying her. He held her close, too close.

As their bodies touched, their eyes locked, both simultaneously experiencing a sense of shock. They exchanged startled glances.

'Is that the only greeting you use, Elaine?' Niall grinned, pleased with the quick recovery he had made. He tried to look casual, but the glint in his eyes said otherwise. 'How about, 'Niall, how lovely to see you.''

'Yes . . . except . . . '

Would that be true? Her heart screamed, 'Yes!' but her head warned, 'No!' This man was like dynamite and her heart felt as though it was about to ignite.

'May I kiss you?'

The words were spoken so softly that Elaine wondered if she had heard aright. The thought made her parted lips curl slightly upwards as her imagination ran through the scenario his words presented.

Niall drew her slightly towards him, so their bodies touched in the water. Elaine's hands were where she had wanted them, her fingers spread out over his chest. As Niall lowered his head and gently covered her mouth with his, her hands rose upwards and outwards until they were sliding over his shoulders and grasping the back of his neck, holding him close.

She had heard others say that time stood still when they were being kissed by the love of their life and she now knew what they meant.

As Niall's lips worked gently against hers, she responded greedily, wanting to be submerged within him, part of him.

It was the cheering cat-calls that eventually caused them to pull apart and grin in embarrassment at the motley spectators.

Elaine felt thoroughly confused. This

man might mean danger to the Malaysian girl, and possibly to herself. What was she doing allowing him to kiss her like that? Was she mad?

She gently wriggled free. There was no point in trying to pretend indignation. Her response had been too obvious for that.

She laughed nervously.

'That was some kiss,' she acknowledged bemusedly.

She frowned, trying to regain some dignity from the situation.

'You didn't answer my question,' she reminded him, glad to put a bit of distance between them.

'Didn't I?' He smiled widely and shrugged his gorgeous shoulders. 'We are booked in here, and you?'

'Well, that's a surprise,' she heard her voice, laced with sarcasm, saying. 'So who followed whom? Your name wasn't in the guest register when we signed in.'

'I think you'll find we were,' Niall drawled. 'We completed a page. Got the last three rooms, though two of our party had to go elsewhere.' He drew her back towards him. 'I don't get the message that you really mind,' he said softly.

'You took me by surprise,' she accused, remembering that attack was the best form of defence. 'I was unprepared.'

Reality suddenly hit her between the eyes. Niall was probably playing a deep and dangerous game. He might think he knew that her response was genuine, but did she know that his was?

'I'll be ready next time,' she quipped lightly.

Niall raised an eyebrow. 'Next time?'

Elaine blushed. She'd walked right into that one.

'Who are you?' she asked seriously.

'I told you, Niall Foster, personnel manager of this lot and many more.'

'Why don't I believe you?'

'I can't help you with that one, honey. All I can say is that I'll try to see you don't get hurt. But, you'll have to trust me.'

Elaine looked up into his face. He was smiling but she detected an underlying seriousness. What exactly did he mean by not get hurt?

Although she found it difficult to believe he would be capable of deliberately hurting anyone, the fear in the Malaysian girl's eyes had been real . . . like that of a hunted animal, she recalled.

Kate was busy chatting to three of Niall's group members. Wise girl, Elaine thought. There was safety in numbers. She joined in with some horseplay and was relieved to see Niall concentrate on doing some fast lengths. His body cleaved through the water with hardly a splash.

But when Niall climbed out on to the side, Elaine had gone.

She was drying her hair in the privacy of her and Kate's room, alternately reliving the intensity of Niall's kiss and desiring a repetition, and telling herself to forget the kiss and Niall altogether.

What on earth had come over her?

Her cheeks felt hot and then cold, as she recalled what had happened in the pool. She didn't always kiss a man on a first date, never mind almost a first encounter.

A battle was raging within her, heart against head . . . and she felt helpless to predict the outcome, all because of that dratted camera.

The sudden thought that she had left the camera untended in their room whilst they had been in the swimming pool caused a stab of alarm. Had anyone been in?

She glanced around. Nothing seemed to have been disturbed and, when she searched in her rucksack, the camera was still there. Burden though it was, she was glad it was still safe.

On an impulse, she put the camera and her money-bag into a plastic bag and slipped down to Reception. Only Mr Williams was there and he was happy to comply with her request that her small package be stored in his safe until morning.

Elaine felt much happier on her return to their room.

When Kate rejoined her ten minutes later and began getting ready, Kate said she had agreed to meet the others at The Black Lion, a well-known restaurant in the town centre.

'I thought we might eat somewhere quietly on our own,' Elaine protested.

'Who is we? You and Niall?'

'No, you and I.'

'No thanks. Your eyes have the glassy look of a girl in love. I don't think I could cope with that all evening.'

'I'm not in love! Kate, this is serious! Niall could be trying to get me on his side. I can't trust him.'

'So, does this let Steve and Phil off the hook? They can't all be after the camera.'

'They all have to remain as suspects until we know for sure.'

'Well, I like Steve. He's good fun.'

'Maybe he is, but don't get too involved too soon.'

The restaurant was already busy

when they arrived, and Elaine discovered that a number of tables had been reserved for their party. The walking group arrived in ones and twos and Elaine manoeuvred herself into a seated position surrounded by early arrivals. She wanted protection from her all-too-willing responses to Niall's charm, she secretly admitted to herself.

Two young women in the group, Rosalyn and Marion, were very friendly.

'What's your rôle within the company?' Elaine asked, hoping to learn something.

'Secretarial,' Marion replied. 'And you?'

'Primary school teacher. What does your company do exactly?'

'We're an international export company. You know, smaller firms who want to sell abroad do so through us, since we already have many outlets all over the world.'

'Oh. Is it interesting?'

Rosalyn pulled a face.

'Sometimes. Mostly it's just routine,

like any other job, I suppose.'

Elaine didn't feel she had got anywhere but didn't like to press further. They were ready to order their meals and conversation settled on discussing the menu.

Elaine wondered where Niall was, wondering how she would be able to hold him at a distance without being too rude about it, but when he eventually arrived with a well-groomed woman on his arm who looked as if she had stepped straight out of a fashion magazine she didn't know whether to be glad or annoyed.

One of the group noticed the direction of her glance.

'That's Amanda Singleton, daughter of the managing director,' he whispered. 'Rumours do abound, if you get my meaning.'

She met Niall's nod of acknowledgement with a brief inclination of her head, relieved that there weren't any spare seats at their particular group of tables, not that Niall made any move in their direction. He guided his partner to an adjoining group, though he did seat himself facing in Elaine's direction.

Elaine fought hard against revealing how much his presence with Miss Singleton had hit her. This was exactly how Marcus had treated her, turning up to the school's summer night out with the daughter of the local director of education. Were all men the same? Marcus had tried to convince her that it was nothing personal . . . all in the cause of swift promotion, he assured her. Huh!

Elaine was the life and soul of the party, and if Niall kept glancing her way with a quizzical expression in his eyes, so much the better.

The arrival of Steve among other diners brought a smile to Kate's face and the group soon shuffled their chairs round to accommodate an extra one. Elaine noticed Niall frowning in Steve's direction but his annoyance only added to her satisfaction that he couldn't ruin everyone's evening.

'Great evening!' Kate declared when they were back in their room at last and getting ready for bed. 'I was a bit surprised with Niall though. Fancy him bringing someone else after the way he was all over you earlier.'

'Couldn't care less, dear!' Elaine lied blithely. 'It made it all the more easy to ignore him. Now, if we can get up early and be amongst the first for breakfast, we'll be able to leave before the group get themselves sorted and we should keep ahead of them all day if we get a move on.'

Kate grinned to herself in the darkness. Unbeknown to Elaine, she had arranged to meet up with Steve later on the next day and the thought of that made her amenable to any other plans. After all, if Elaine could have a bit of romance on the holiday, so could she.

Their plan worked to perfection. A note slipped under their door invited both girls to an early-morning swim in the pool but, although reluctant to miss the opportunity of starting the day in the refreshing water, Elaine insisted that they disregard the invitation.

As they settled their overnight bill, she asked for the return of her small package and thrust it deep inside her rucksack once more.

The weather seemed changeable so they were delighted to set off in dry weather and left Hay-On-Wye by the bridge over the river. A riverside walk took them a few miles away from the town and over a stile engraved with the statement that Prestatyn was one hundred and twenty-three miles away.

Open fields, areas of woodland, countless styles and short stretches along a B-road eventually brought them in mid-afternoon to The Royal Oak, their booked B&B, only to be confronted by an apologetic landlord.

'I'm sorry, girls. We've had a leak in the room we'd laid aside for you both, but don't worry,' he said as he saw their faces fall with the prospect of nowhere to spend the night. 'I've fixed you up with my daughter, Janice, who lives on a farm a few miles up the road. I'll run you over there and, in the morning, my daughter will run you back here so that you don't miss any mileage. I know what you walkers are like over missed miles!'

His daughter's stone-built farm was off the beaten track. It was fully modernised inside and the room they were given was large and airy. Since she offered to cook them an evening meal, they stayed in all evening, instead of following their usual practice of finding a nearby pub or restaurant. As if to compensate for what might have been regarded as a let-down from their original booking, she offered them a riding lesson.

Since neither of them had ever ridden, this was a chance not to miss and they had a hilarious time learning to mount and then stay put on their horses' backs.

'That was great, Janice. Thank you!' both girls declared when they finally slithered to the ground. 'Now, a hot bath to ease our aching muscles!'

Kate spared a momentary thought for Steve, wondering if he would be disappointed when she didn't meet him later in The Royal Oak but couldn't think of a good enough excuse to tell Elaine why she needed to leave a message for him. She should have thought earlier and scribbled a message whilst they were there but she consoled herself with the thought that he would understand when she told him, if she saw him again that was.

The following morning, they were greeted by an agitated Janice, who hustled them into the dining-room to start their breakfast as early as possible.

'My dad's place was burgled last night!' she explained breathlessly.

6

'Most of the rooms were entered and guests' baggage rifled through,' Janice went on. 'They must have been professionals because no-one was disturbed and it only became clear this morning when people realised that things weren't quite as they left them. You had a lucky escape there. The funny thing is, Dad said that nothing seems to have been taken.'

Elaine's first thought was about the camera hidden at the bottom of her rucksack. Was that what the intruders were after? It might not have been but the thought made her uneasy.

Janice took them back to The Royal Oak and dashed inside to see her dad, leaving Elaine and Kate outside. A couple of police cars were parked at one side. The officers were talking to the guests whose belongings had been disturbed.

The thought of the camera in her rucksack weighed heavily on Elaine's mind. Was there any point in mentioning it to the police?

No. She hadn't enough to tell them.

Two walkers were fastening their boot laces, rucksacks ready to be hitched on to their backs.

'Hi, guys!' Kate greeted them. 'It seems we missed the excitement.'

'Lucky you. It's a bit unnerving to know someone has been in your room whilst you were asleep.'

'Yes, I can well imagine,' Elaine sympathised. 'Er, was there a large group of walkers here last night?'

'No, just us and a few other guys and a couple of women. You lost someone?'

'No, no. I just wondered. We were at the same place the day before yesterday and we didn't ask them how far they were going yesterday.'

'I think they were going on to Kington,' the other walker offered.

Kington was about five miles farther on. It seemed they weren't far apart then, except she and Kate were now four or five miles behind. Well, that suited her. They would be able to spot them ahead and adjust their pace accordingly.

Their route that day was along Hergest Ridge, giving glorious views of the surrounding moors and woodland. They were hoping to pass through Kington just before lunch but when they emerged out of St Mary's churchyard via the lych gate and entered the town, Elaine was disappointed to discover that the post office was already closed.

Although she had no proof that the burglary in Gladestry was an attempt to get hold of the camera, it had persuaded her that the camera needed to be more safely guarded. She had thought long and hard about it during the morning walk and had come to the conclusion that the best thing to do would be to buy a padded envelope and post the camera to their final B&B before Prestatyn.

Before she was able to tell Kate about her decision, a male voice hailed them from by The Swan, a pub in the town square. It was Steve.

'Hi!' he called. 'I wondered if I'd see you girls today.' He spoke to both of them but it was Kate to whom he directed his brilliant smile. 'Sorry I didn't make it to Gladestry yesterday. I met up with an interesting guy from Australia and we made a lunchtime diversion to a village pub.'

'You still managed to get to Kington before us,' Elaine said sharply, still not trusting anyone who seemed to be trailing them.

'Elaine!' Kate reproved her, embarrassed by her tone.

Steve laughed, spreading his hands in admission of being caught out.

'Cheated, I'm afraid! We got a lift into town.'

Kate glared at Elaine and took great delight in linking her arm into Steve's.

'I could do with a drink, you know. We were very chaste ourselves last night since we ended up on a farm miles from anywhere. And, you'll never guess what happened . . . '

As they made their way to The Swan, Elaine heard her sister telling Steve all about the night's happenings at The Royal Oak.

They ordered a sandwich and a drink each and took them over to a corner table to eat them in comfort. Kate eventually excused herself and wriggled out of her seat to make her way to the ladies. Steve lowered his glass to the table as he watched her go. He then turned towards Elaine and slid across the seat towards her.

'Look, Elaine, I know you don't like me for some reason. We must have got off to a bad start somehow, though all I did was restore your camera to you. Not a very big crime, was it?'

He paused, as if he didn't quite know how to continue and then touched her arm.

'Don't take me wrong in what I'm about to say, I just feel I have to warn you.'

'Warn me?' Elaine repeated. 'What do you mean?'

Steve glanced about them quickly, as if making sure that he wasn't about to be overheard. He made a slight grimace of displeasure and then spoke in a lowered tone.

'It's about Niall Foster. I can't help noticing that you seem to be quite taken with him. I used . . . '

'No, I'm not!' Elaine denied swiftly. 'I've only just met him. I hardly know him.'

'That's what I mean,' Steve said quietly. 'The fact is, I do know him. I used to work at the same place. There was something a bit dodgy going on in high places, if you know what I mean. Foster made life very difficult for me, so, I got out of it whilst the going was good.'

He looked earnestly at Elaine.

'Don't always trust what he says, that's all. He's great at leading you up the path while it suits his purpose.'

Elaine felt her spirits sink. How right

he was! Steve didn't know how well he had summed up what had already happened between them. But, could she trust Steve?

'How do I know . . . ?' she began.

' . . . that you can trust me?' Steve finished for her. 'You don't! But I've no axe to grind. I like Kate and, since you're her sister, I just felt I had to warn you before you get hurt. That's all. Take it or leave it, it's all the same to me.'

Kate was on her way back and Steve slid back to his original place.

'I've been sweet-talking your sister,' he said lightly, swinging his glance to include Elaine. 'I think we've cleared the air a bit, haven't we, Elaine?'

'Sort of,' Elaine agreed.

She felt perturbed. Was it just a friendly piece of advice, as he wanted her to believe? It wasn't as if he had anything personal to gain from turning her against Niall. It was Kate he seemed interested in, not her.

Phil's appearance made a welcome

diversion. With the easy comradeship of long-distance walkers, he joined their small group without waiting to be invited.

Both young men were pleasant enough on the surface, and Elaine would have normally enjoyed their company in a light-hearted, non-committed way. As it was, she was too apprehensive of what Kate might unthinkingly let slip and she tried to read undercurrents in any questions that were asked.

Her uneasiness wasn't helped when Niall and his party strolled into the pub and spread themselves amongst the seating arrangements in the lounge. A chorus of greetings rang out but Elaine avoided making eye contact with Niall, regretting her willingness to kiss him in the pool at Hay-on-Wye and still annoyed by his later public ignoring of her.

Elaine wouldn't have been surprised to learn that Niall also regretted his impulsive action of kissing her so passionately, but she might have been surprised by the reason for his regret. Seeing her again did nothing to ease Niall's conscience but he had to admit that it was fortunate that Amanda had appeared when she had. She had given him a cover for his stepping away from the situation, even though it meant a public rejection of Elaine.

Was Elaine as unmoved as she seemed? It was entirely his own fault and he could only blame himself for his lack of self-control. How often had he lectured new recruits on the necessity of self-control at all times!

He had never before acted so recklessly during an assignment . . . indeed had never even felt inclined to do so since Magdala, his wife, had died so tragically of cancer four years ago, taking their unborn child with her. His life had been left so empty that for over eighteen months he had retreated into a cold, dark world that his friends had thought would hold him for ever.

Time had eventually eased his outer

grief and he had gradually begun to pick himself up again. He had grown to revel in danger both in work and play. His heart, however, had remained untouched by the few casual relationships he had had since then. Magdala had spoiled him for the seeming blandness of other women.

So, what was it about Elaine that attracted him so much? Was it merely a physical attraction? He didn't think so, though she was pretty enough to catch any man's eye.

A nudge at his elbow brought him back to reality.

'Are we having another?' Grant Hodges asked.

Niall flickered his glance to the corner where Elaine and Kate were laughing at something Steve Martin had just said. His gaze lasted a fraction too long and he was aware that Elaine had sensed his interest. He could see the hurt in her eyes, though she swiftly drew a veil over them and she turned to speak to Steve over her shoulder.

He wished he could explain to her that his kisses had been real . . . had meant so much that he had been in danger of blowing his cover and ruining the whole operation. But he couldn't, because that would blow his cover also. And, in spite of the intensity of attraction between them, he still wasn't sure of her reason for being involved in this nasty business, nor did he know the depth of her involvement.

Was she with them or against them? Part of the conspiracy or somehow innocently caught up in it? Until he was sure of where their allegiance lay, he couldn't let them know of his involvement.

The one thing he did know, or, at least, strongly suspected, was that Elaine had the camera. He had to get it off her.

He got to his feet, angling his body so that his lip movements couldn't be read by anyone else.

'Have you found out where they're staying tonight?' he asked Grant.

'Yes. A private house at Discoed. We've managed to book four of us in the same place.'

'Good. What about Steve Martin?'

'He's not booked in anywhere so he'll have to try elsewhere,' Grant spoke with barely a movement of his lips and his eyes warned Niall not to reply.

Niall bent down to pick up his rucksack, nodding briefly as Elaine, Kate, Phil and Steve filed past on their way to the door. When they had gone outside, he continued his conversation with Grant.

'What about the new chap?'

'He's called Phil. From what I've gathered, they met at Tintern Abbey and haven't seen him since Llanthony. Kate openly told him about their camera being stolen and, surprisingly, of its return by Steve Martin the following day. It was obvious that Elaine didn't like the incident being spoken about.'

Niall's right eyebrow had risen. So, she still had two cameras, both presumably near enough alike to be confused with the other.

He clenched his fists in frustration. Was she a courier or not? If only he knew!

'Let's be off, then. I don't want to lose sight of them for too long.'

They crossed the square and turned down by the old national school and then down to the pretty area of Crooked Well, where a cluster of old lime-washed cottages nestled together near a duck-inhabited stream.

Niall could see the group of walkers up ahead and satisfied himself that Elaine and Kate were well-surrounded by his own men.

They were approaching a golf course when he finally caught up with Elaine. She had dropped behind her sister, who was chatting animatedly to Steve. Phil had attached himself to one of Niall's group and they were in the midst of a heated political discussion that seemed to fuel their energy as they strode up the sleep incline.

As Elaine broke clear of the protection of tall bushes and into the open, a shout of, 'Fore!' brought her to a sudden standstill. She turned her head in the direction of the shout and sensed the presence of a missile whizzing past her at head height. She leaped backwards, straight into Niall's arms.

He pulled her to him, twisting his body round so that he was shielding her from the green, which lay far below.

'Are you all right?' he asked, gently disengaging her.

Elaine nodded, now feeling embarrassed by her nervous reaction.

'Yes. I'd forgotten we were approaching a golf course!' She laughed shakily.

She deliberately stepped away from him, noticing that he made no move to restrain her.

'You're still following us, I see,' she challenged him, raising her eyes to meet his for the first time.

She was surprised to see a flicker of . . . she almost thought, tenderness, but when she concentrated her gaze, she knew she had been mistaken. There was nothing there but casual interest.

'Kington is a very hospitable place,' he praised lightly. 'I decided that my group needed a brief respite.'

'I thought the whole idea of these venture weeks was to put the group into unknown territory and let them discover their true self,' Elaine challenged again, slightly sarcastically.

'True,' Niall allowed, 'but I don't want to overdo it, not at this stage, anyway.'

'Mmm, well, Kate and I aren't in your group, so you needn't keep an eye on us,' Elaine said tartly, though not in ill-humour.

'I'll try to remember that,' Niall responded, with laughter in his voice.

Elaine was very conscious of his closeness and wondered if his heart was beating as fast as hers was. It was insane! This man was dangerous!

Niall sighed softly and half-turned her towards him. Was he going to kiss her again? She felt torn between being sure she would be angry if he did and dying if he didn't!

Niall's eyes held hers and he seemed to sense her uncertainty.

'You are a lovely young woman,' he breathed softly. 'And very kissable. But I don't want to hurt you. Maybe . . . '

'Come on, you two!'

The shout from one of the others stopped whatever he was going to say and their eyes were drawn away from each other.

Niall grinned ruefully, rubbing his chin.

'It's the wrong time . . . and the wrong place,' he said, more to himself than to Elaine.

Elaine was pleased that the tension between them had melted a little. She would simply have to bear in mind Steve's warning and make sure that they kept their interaction on a light footing in future.

As the afternoon was drawing on, Elaine knew that they would soon be approaching her planned diversion to their night's B&B but before she could mention this, Niall signalled a halt.

'I'm afraid four of our party bow out here.' He waved his hand across the fields to where a few roofs could be seen above the tops of some trees and bushes. 'The rest of you . . . '

Elaine swiftly consulted her map. 'But this is where Kate and I will leave as well.' She glared suspiciously at Niall. 'We're staying at Woodwinds.'

'Well, of all the coincidences. So are we! Look!' He held out his guide book with a signed receipt for his deposit stapled to the relevant page. 'Unfortunately, Mrs Ambridge could only take four of us, so the rest are continuing to Dolley Green, where we'll all reassemble tomorrow at ten o'clock. Is that OK, folks?'

He addressed his own party and seemed oblivious to Kate's dismay.

'Oh, dear, Steve! That rules out your hope of getting a bed there. What will you do?' she asked.

'Oh, I think I'll still come and chance it.'

'I wouldn't count on it,' Niall warned. 'I made the same suggestion to Mrs Ambridge but she said it would be a waste of time. Otherwise, we'd have stayed together. Where are you heading, Phil?'

'I got in at Maes-Treylow. You'd best come with me, Steve, and we'll see these guys on the road.'

With a wave of his hand, Phil set off along the path, followed by the remainder of Niall's group and lastly by a reluctant Steve.

'Well, I must say that was a bit hard on Steve. Couldn't one of your lot let him have a bed?' Kate directed at Niall.

Niall shrugged his shoulders.

'He should have booked in if he wanted to be sure of a bed. You did. We did. With a group this size, it would be bad planning not to do so. I owe it to my group.'

Elaine frowned. Niall seemed to have successfully separated her and Kate from Steve and Phil. Was it by chance?

Or did he have a reason?

7

With the thought that Niall might have an ulterior motive in splitting the two men from them, Elaine fell into line behind him and his three companions. Kate had hung back for a few moments, no doubt sharing a hasty kiss with Steve, but she was now trudging behind her.

Elaine had had grave suspicions about Steve and, to a lesser extent, about Phil being somehow connected with the Malaysian girl's distress and disappearance, but she was equally certain that Niall was also connected.

Their paths had crossed far too often for them to be pure coincidences. Twice, she could have bought, three times, even! But . . . how many had it been? She cast her mind and did a rapid count. It was five or six. Could they all be mere coincidences?

When had Niall's party set off? There had been no indication that Niall was intending to walk the path until after they had bumped into each other in Monmouth.

But, if it hadn't already been planned, how did he manage to scrape the other eight together so quickly? No, it had to be a genuine, organised group, didn't it?

She thought about Niall's present three companions . . . Pete, Rosalyn and Marion. She hadn't spoken much to Pete, he seemed fairly quiet, but Rosalyn and Marion were easy to talk to, so the evening promised to be a congenial one.

Mrs Ambridge and a huge black dog greeted their guests with a hearty welcome.

'Come in! Come in! Down, Boris! These are friends! Let him sniff your hands and then he'll know you are invited guests. That's it, Boris. Now, out you go into the garden.'

She closed the door behind him and

turned back to her six guests.

'Now, tell me who's who. Who are the two Miss Driscoes?'

'We are.' Elaine smiled, indicating her and Kate.

'Right! Now, as you know, I had planned to put you in the apartment over the garage. I think I mentioned it when you booked, didn't I? But, if it's all the same to you, I think we'll put the two men in there and you can join the other two ladies in the house. Is that all right by you?'

'Yes, fine,' Elaine agreed. So, they had booked before Niall.

Mrs Armitage appraised the state of their clothes.

'Mmm, you all look quite dry and mud-free. Off with your boots, then, and just deposit your rucksacks in your rooms. Then, you can join me in the lounge through there. I'm sure you'll all be ready for a slice of this!'

She produced a huge, treble-layered carrot cake, held together with cream. It looked sinfully mouth-watering.

When they returned to the lounge, the cake had been divided into large portions and a large pot of tea stood ready to be poured.

'Let's have a photo then, Elaine!' Rosalyn demanded.

Elaine jumped, her hand hesitating at the cord around her neck. The moment seemed to stretch into minutes as she frantically tried to think of a reasonable-sounding excuse. She really didn't want to use the Malaysian girl's camera. It didn't seem the right thing to do.

'E . . . I need a new . . . '

'It's jammed,' Kate said simultaneously.

Rescue came from a surprising quarter. Niall unzipped a side-pocket and produced his own camera, a neat-looking digital one.

'Let's use mine. We'll be able to see the result immediately and you can all put in your orders. So, squash together a bit more and look this way. And you, too, Mrs Armitage.'

Dizzy with relief, Elaine took her

place with the others gathered around their hostess, all pretending to take a huge bite from their slice of cake.

'I'll take one with you in it now,' Mrs Armitage offered.

They posed once more, repeating the charade of eating the cake . . . and then tucked in hungrily. It tasted as wonderful as it looked.

'Would you like copies of the photographs when I get them printed, Elaine and Kate?' Niall asked casually.

'You bet!' Kate agreed enthusiastically.

Elaine was suddenly suspicious. Was it a ruse to get hold of their address?

His eyes met hers. He was smiling, not only with his lips but his eyes, too. She wasn't sure what message she was reading in them. Did he know Steve had warned her off him? Was it assurance that she could trust him?

She was grateful for his intervention in offering his camera to be used. He could have let Rosalyn keep her in the spotlight. What harm would there be in letting him have it? He didn't know that the house was standing empty whilst their parents were on holiday, in fact, she would let him think they were there.

She held out her hand for the piece of notepaper and wrote their address.

'It's our parents' house,' she stated casually. 'We still live at home.'

'I'll give you mine,' Niall offered, as he wrote it down.

Despite Steve's warning, Elaine thrilled at the touch of his hand as they exchanged papers. Did he feel it, too?

Niall picked up his plate and made pretence of eating, in reality watching Elaine as she ate. His fingers had ached to caress her hand. It had taken his full self-control not to seize hold of her hand as she had pulled it away. He was sure she had felt the spark between them when their hands had touched.

She was lovely. His heart ached. What were they doing to her? What might they do to her if this wasn't ended soon? They couldn't go on like this.

They had to get the camera, and he was pretty sure Elaine had it.

He didn't know why he thought that. Instinct, he supposed, that seventh sense that had saved his bacon on more than one occasion. She was nervous . . . closed in . . . wary. That was surely the reason why she hadn't wanted to use it to take their photograph. If it had been her own, she would have pulled it out like a shot. He'd seen her taking enough photographs to know that.

If only he could get it off her without her being aware of his involvement with it, he could wait a while, a few months, maybe, and then get in touch with her, as if by accident, perhaps. Or would the nature of his involvement be a permanent barrier between them? He'd seen enough marriages among his colleagues hit the rocks to know the danger of that.

He was suddenly shaken by his thoughts. Marriage? He hardly knew the girl. No, he couldn't contemplate getting married again, not unless he was prepared to give up his risky life-style, and he wasn't convinced that he ever would. He needed the buzz.

His contemplations were interrupted by Mrs Armitage's return to the room.

'If you've all had enough to eat, I'll shoo you all away to do whatever it is you walkers do to spruce yourselves up,' she said briskly. 'Dinner is at seven. Off you go now and let me get the table ready. Oh, and if any of you wants to do any washing, you can use the washing-machine in the utility room just off the kitchen.'

All four young women hurriedly decided to take the opportunity to wash their clothes and Elaine volunteered to take the collection of labelled bags downstairs, surreptitiously taking with her the small parcel of her moneybag and the camera. Anxious not to suggest that she didn't trust Rosalyn or Marion, she used the excuse of her nervousness after the burglary at The Royal Oak.

'Have no fear,' Mrs Armitage assured her. 'This house is fully alarmed. And don't forget Boris. It'll be a foolhardy burglar who tries to break in here.'

Dinner was beautifully cooked and tasted delicious. Afterwards, the six guests played a selection of board games.

It was nearly midnight when they reluctantly decided to call it a day, groaning at the thought of rising for breakfast in about seven hours' time.

They were awakened long before that, when the all-efficient burglar alarm sounded its warning.

As loud barks from Boris sounded from the garden, Elaine sat up and ran her fingers through her hair. Her brain slowly woke up.

'It's the burglar alarm. Someone's broken in!'

She leaped out of bed, pulling the light-weight duvet round her shoulders to cover her nightwear and opened the bedroom door. Rosalyn was already on the landing and Marion quickly joined them.

Mrs Armitage appeared, hair in rollers.

'Aha! What did I tell you! Follow me. There's safety in numbers.'

She led the way downstairs fearlessly, brandishing what looked like an old rounders stick in her hand.

Mrs Armitage went straight to the control panel of her alarm system.

'It's the apartment over the garage,' she announced.

'Don't you think we should wait for the police?' Elaine suggested.

'Nonsense! It'll take them half-an-hour to get here. One of you stay here and lock the door after us. You, young lady.' She indicated Rosalyn. 'And make sure the downstairs rooms are secure.'

Marion darted outside and ran towards the sound of Boris's barking. Elaine and Kate followed Mrs Armitage into the garden, arriving just as Niall and Pete reached the foot of the external stairway from their apartment over the garage. Boris was leaping up at the fence, barking excitedly. Luckily for the intruder, Boris's high-jump attempts failed.

'He got away!' Mrs Armitage exclaimed, deep disappointment in her voice. 'Never mind! Well done, Boris! Good boy!'

She patted his head and then turned to Niall and Pete.

'Where did he try to get in?'

'It must have been a downstairs window. If Boris had caught him on the external staircase, he'd have had him for supper by now,' Niall stated, a hint of humour in his voice as he responded to Mrs Armitage's reaction. 'Let's look around, Pete.'

The two men set off around the back of the detached building and Mrs Armitage and Boris set off in the other direction.

'We'll check round the house,' Marion offered, nodding at Elaine and Kate. 'You two go that way and I'll go this way.' She set off at a steady jog.

Elaine and Kate ran the other way, admiring Marion's nerve in going alone. They met Marion around at the front of the house.

'There's no sign of anything having

been disturbed in the main house,' Marion assured them. 'I expect the intruder thought the garage and apartment is a self-contained cottage. With it having windows and a side-door like it has, it looks like that, doesn't it?'

Niall, Pete and Mrs Armitage reappeared, having discovered the break-in site.

'The window around the other side was forced,' Niall said, by way of explanation to Elaine. 'It only leads into the downstairs garage. There's no connecting internal door, so it can be safely left until daylight.'

Elaine shivered. She couldn't help thinking that she and Kate should have been in the apartment over the garage. Was this a second foiled attempt at getting the camera off her?

And who had the intruder been? Who might know that she and Kate should have been up there? Could it have been another of Niall's party? But, if Niall had contacted them on his mobile phone, he'd have told them that Elaine and Kate were in the house. The intruder wouldn't have tried to break into the garage.

They returned to the main house and Rosalyn reported that the main house hadn't been touched. Mrs Armitage put on the kettle.

Elaine couldn't wait to get alone with Kate to ask her a very pertinent question.

'Did you tell Steve where we'd be sleeping?'

'Of course not!' Kate denied vehemently.

'Well, it's strange that the burglar tried to get into the apartment and not the main house.'

'How do you know the burglar was after that stupid camera? You're obsessed with it.'

'It has to be. He's tried twice.'

'But that doesn't mean it has to be Steve! He brought your camera back, remember. It could be your precious Niall.'

'He isn't my precious Niall. He isn't

my anything. Anyway, how could it have been Niall? He was with Pete.'

'So?'

Suddenly, it occurred to Elaine that there was another possibility. The attempted break-in might have been a diversion to get them all out of their rooms, leaving Rosalyn free to search their rucksacks. Well, if so, the plan had been thwarted by her giving the camera into Mrs Armitage's care.

She voiced her thoughts to Kate.

Kate considered for a moment.

'Then they're all in it,' she said slowly, 'Pete, Rosalyn and Marion, and the rest. They have to be,' Kate added.

Elaine sank on to the bed.

'I can't take it in. What's it all about?'

'I don't know.' Kate sat beside her. 'I think we should ditch the camera at the first opportunity. It's getting too scary.'

'Then what? It would still go on. No-one would know I no longer had it.'

Kate whirled to her feet and paced up and down.

'Then have a confrontation. Tip out

your rucksack and invite them to go through it. Show them it's not there.' She paused and held out her hand. 'Give it to me! I'll throw it out first thing in the morning.'

Elaine shook her head.

'I haven't actually got it right now. I gave it to Mrs Armitage to mind for me, but you're right. I'll have to do something about it. But not tonight.' She sighed wearily. 'Let's get back to bed. We've a long trek tomorrow.'

Elaine didn't find it easy to fall back asleep. It must have been the same for everyone else as well, as they all looked a bit bleary-eyed when they gathered for breakfast.

Elaine had warned Kate not to say anything about their part in it all.

'Even if you're right and Niall and his group are in on it all, they can't be sure about us. They would have done something more definite about it if they were. We must let them go on wondering.'

'What will you do with it?'

'I'm still thinking about it. It might be best if you don't know.'

'Don't you trust me?'

Elaine hugged her.

'Of course I do, silly. It's just that if you don't know, you can't let it slip.'

Conversation around the breakfast table tended to be on more general items, as if everyone was afraid of saying the wrong thing.

Even Mrs Armitage only referred to the previous night's events to remark, 'I've given all your home addresses to the police in case they need to check up on you. I don't suppose they will though. There's too many attempted break-ins. They only want to know about the successful ones.'

There seemed to be a changed atmosphere among the six walkers, the friendliness of the previous evening evaporating in the morning sun. Elaine felt as though Niall and the other three closed around her and Kate, though whether in escort or citizen arrest, she couldn't be sure.

They met up with the remainder of Niall's party as arranged at Dolley Green just before ten o'clock and they soon told the others of their night-time adventure. Suspicious as she was about the nature of the group, Elaine found herself smiling sceptically at their gasps of concern and surprise.

There was no sign of Steve and Phil and she wondered if her suspicions of them were indeed unfounded. It seemed more than likely.

Walking through the fields, full of either sheep or thigh-high corn, was very pleasant, with exceptional views of the Malverns to the south-east and the Brecon Beacons to the south-west, especially when they were once more on top of long stretches of the dyke.

The walkers chatted sociably as they trudged along, changing walking part-ners on a whim and drifting into companionable silences as they silently drank in the peace and beauty of their surroundings.

It made their situation seem even

more unreal, and Elaine began to question if she was letting her imagination run along the lines of late-night thrillers. Whilst her thoughts tumbled around in her mind, she strode out strongly and it was quite a while before she realised that she had out-stripped the others.

Pausing, she placed her hands in the small of her back and rolled her shoulders backwards, easing her neck muscles. The path was quite high up and she had a panoramic view of the valley below.

She decided to take the opportunity for a quiet sit while she drank in the tranquil scene, so she shrugged off her rucksack and sank on to the soft grass at the edge of the rise, stretching her legs down the slope in front of her.

Having drunk one bottle of water, she rummaged in the side pocket of her rucksack for her other and put the empty one in its place. She selected an apple to eat while she waited for the others to catch up with her.

What should she do? There was no-one to talk things over with, except Kate, and Kate was inclined to treat the matter too lightly and was likely to unintentionally chat about it to Steve.

So engrossed was she in her thoughts that she wasn't aware of anyone approaching her from behind until a sixth sense warned her that someone was near. As she began to turn her head to see who it was, a hefty shove in the middle of her back sent her toppling off balance. Her arms shot out, instinctively reaching for something to hold on to. Her right hand made contact with her rucksack strap, realising too late that it wasn't going to prevent her falling. Nevertheless her fingers clasped round it.

Over and over, she tumbled down the grassy slope, unable to stop herself. Time seemed endless. She knew she had screamed as she began to fall but now she had no breath to spare as each rotation squeezed her remaining breath out of her.

At last she could feel herself slowing down and managed to grab hold of a handful of grass. It came away in her hand but had slowed her sufficiently for her to grab again. This time, the grass held and she found herself lying face down against the grassy slope.

She lay winded, her heart thumping against her ribs. Nothing hurt, though she knew she would feel it later.

She tried to recall exactly what she had seen, but there was nothing, simply an impression that someone had crept up behind her and sent her sprawling down the slope.

Her rucksack? Where was it?

She slowly pushed herself up on to her knees and looked upwards. All she could see was grass and sky. She twisted round.

There it was.

Her rucksack had bounded on down the slope and lay twenty metres or so below her. Lying flat, she rolled sideways in a controlled roll down towards her rucksack. She flopped beside it and rested again.

'Elaine!'

It was Niall's voice. Her mind froze. Had he been the one to push her? He was the first on the scene.

'Keep still! I'm coming!'

Elaine raised her head and she could see him bounding diagonally down the slope towards her.

'Are you all right, Elaine?' he asked, deep concern in his voice.

For a moment, she couldn't speak. She swallowed hard.

'Yes. Yes, I think so.'

She pushed herself up into a sitting position, wincing as her body protested.

'You haven't broken anything, have you? Here, let me feel.'

Elaine jerked her body away.

'I'm all right!' she snapped.

'OK. That's fine. Do you think you can stand?'

'Of course!'

Niall held out his hand but Elaine ignored it and struggled to her feet.

Niall grimaced wryly. One thing, she had pluck.

'I'll carry your rucksack,' he offered.

'No!'

Niall placed his hands on her shoulders and looked her squarely in her eyes.

'I just want to help you back up the slope. The others are waiting up there.'

He raised his head. He couldn't see the top of the slope but he could see Kate gingerly coming down.

'It's all right, Kate,' he called. 'Elaine's fine. Wait there! We'll come up as soon as Elaine gets her breath back.'

He looked down at Elaine. He wanted to take her in his arms, but that would sidetrack him and he'd almost gone that way already. If only all this ghastly business were over and they could start again, if that were possible. She didn't seem too pleased to see him right now. In fact she was glaring quite ferociously at him.

'What happened, Elaine?' he asked.

'Someone pushed me!' Elaine said

tersely, stepping back a little.

'Who was it? Did you see who it was?'

She shook her head. 'No, but I wasn't mistaken.'

Niall understood her mistrust of him. He smiled gently.

'It wasn't me, Elaine. You must know I wouldn't hurt you like that.'

He saw doubt and hope flicker across her face but knew he couldn't help her to choose which one she would seize hold of.

'Elaine! Are you all right?'

It was Kate shouting down again, her tone of voice showing her anxiety.

Elaine glanced upwards. She was feeling her breath coming more easily and her heartbeat had steadied but she wasn't sure she had the energy to climb back to where the others were waiting.

She looked reluctantly at Niall, shrugging her shoulders in resignation.

'I'll accept your help,' she said primly.

8

It was just before lunchtime when they entered Knighton, the mid-point of the Offa's Dyke Path and where the Offa's Dyke Association had their headquarters.

Elaine felt that she had walked off some of the stiffness caused by the fall but she was now determined to get rid of the camera. However, she had decided that although she eventually wanted Niall and the others to know she no longer had it, she didn't want them to know how she had got rid of it, therefore she needed an excuse to visit the post office. When planning the walk, she had weighed the maps and guide books and had a ready-stamped, self-addressed envelope for sending them home as they became redundant at Knighton, but only Kate knew that.

'I'm going to send the first guidebook

home,' Elaine announced to all who were nearby. 'I'll send home the maps we've finished with, as well. It will all help to lighten the load.'

She darted into the post office. Rosalyn had followed her in but Elaine was sure she hadn't seen that the envelope she bought was a padded one. She also made sure Rosalyn couldn't see what she wrote on the front of the envelope, and then delved into her rucksack for the ready-addressed one. She pushed the camera into the padded one and then flourished the one with the guide book already in it.

'I won't be a minute, Rosalyn,' she called.

When she reached the head of the queue, she placed the one with the camera in it on to the weighing scales and then carefully stuck on the stamps. Using her body as a shield, she slid the camera parcel into the parcel box. Whew, that was a relief!

When she rejoined Rosalyn, she had only the slimmer parcel in her hand.

'Be a love and drop this in the box for me while I fasten up my rucksack,' she said to Rosalyn.

She didn't miss the appraising look the parcel was given.

They quickly met with the others by the old clock tower in the middle of Broad Street. Elaine saw at once that Steve had joined the group once more and that Kate was animatedly telling him about the attempted break-in and her tumble down the fell side.

They decided to visit the Offa's Dyke Association Information Office in West Street on their way out of town.

Before leaving the information centre a little while later, Elaine insisted on taking a photograph of the whole group with the camera hanging on it's cord around her neck in order to dispel any suspicions that it might be the much sought-after camera. That done, they went straight on to a riverside path until they reached the bridge.

Kate and Steve had drawn ahead, as had three or four of the others, and they were already on the other side. Some cows were drinking at the river's edge and were congregated near the end of the bridge. Elaine found their close presence a bit intimidating and hastily stepped to her right as one of the cows lifted its head towards her.

Maybe she was still unsteady from her morning tumble, whatever, the next thing she knew she had lost her footing and was slipping, falling, rolling into the river.

It wasn't deep at the edge of the river at that point but she had been fully submerged before she managed to splutter her way to her knees and then her feet, feeling an absolute fool.

Niall was already standing in the river beside her, shooing away a curious cow that obviously wanted a closer look at this strange creature sharing their waterway.

With his left hand under her left elbow and the other around her back taking the weight of her rucksack, he managed to hold her steady and push her upwards. Grant was on the bank, his hand grasping hold of Elaine's right hand. Between them, she was hoisted back on to the river bank.

'Ugh! That was an unwelcome bath!' she exclaimed, trying to laugh lightly, although, inside, she was shaking.

'Your camera's got wet, I'm afraid,' Marion sympathised. 'Your film will be ruined.'

'You'd better see if your spare clothes are still dry and change into them,' Niall advised. 'Have you got everything in a plastic inner bag?'

'Yes, and everything in separate plastic bags inside that. We've learned the hard way about keeping our clothes dry.'

'I think you'd better go back to the information centre,' Niall suggested. 'A few of us will wait here for you. The rest had better catch up with those in front and let them know about the delay.'

'I'll come with you, Elaine,' Marion offered.

'I'll come as well,' Rosalyn volunteered.

Elaine saw Niall and Marion make eye contact, followed by an almost indiscernible nod of their heads. Her lips tightened and she felt a sense of betrayal. Well, they might be thinking this had played into their hands by giving them the possibility of a chance to examine her rucksack, but it was exactly what she had wanted. She couldn't have planned it better if she had tried.

The three young women trudged back to the information centre. Elaine's boots squelching with every step. They were greeted with sympathetic smiles and the offer of hand towels and they crossed over to the toilets.

Elaine shrugged her rucksack off her back and lowered it to the floor. After she'd undone the buckles and pulled open the main compartment, she rummaged inside for two of the smaller plastic bags that held her spare underwear, shorts and T-shirt.

'Do me a favour, girls,' she said, as she went into one of the cubicles. 'Tip

139

everything out for me and make sure none of the bags has let water in, especially the main inner lining. You'd better do the side pockets, too.'

Elaine concentrated on stripping off her wet clothes, rubbing herself down and putting on the dry clothes. She eventually emerged into the general area with her wet clothes in her hand. Marion was on her own.

'Oh, has Rosalyn gone?'

'Yes, she's buying some postcards she'd forgotten to get. I told her to catch up with the others and tell them we won't be long.'

Hmm. Messenger reporting, no camera, Elaine conjectured silently.

'I'll put these into a plastic bag and hope Mrs Reynolds at tonight's B&B will let me wash and dry them. We've found most of our landladies very helpful. Have you?'

'Yes. They're great. I don't suppose they'd be doing it if they weren't.'

They both laughed as Elaine re-packed her rucksack.

'Is everything dry?'

'Yes. You've done well there. There's nothing worse than finding your night-wear wet after a weary trudge through wind and rain, is there?'

'No, you're right. We saw a father and his son give up on the Pennine Way when they found everything soaked. At least in the glorious weather of the past couple of days, we've had no problems there. Which day did you set out, by the way? Did you get very wet at first?'

'Er . . . no . . . er . . . '

For the first time, Elaine saw Marion discomfited as she hesitated over their commencement date and whether or not it had rained heavily.

'Monday . . . er . . . no . . . Sunday, it was,' she amended hastily. She laughed. 'We lose track of the days on a holiday like this, don't we? It all becomes, day one, day two, and so on.'

'Yes. So, today's day six,' Elaine agreed craftily, aware that for her and Kate it was day eight, counting their travelling day.

'Er . . . yes, day six,' Marion repeated hesitatingly.

Elaine smiled inwardly, knowing it should have been at least day seven if they had all started at Chepstow. They had first seen Niall on their first day and again on day three in Monmouth. They hadn't seen the rest of the group until Hay-On-Wye on their fifth day. She'd lay money on that being their first day.

'What about my camera? Did that get very wet, do you think?' she now asked as she picked it up. 'Do you think I'd better open it up and look inside?'

'You'll lose your film, if you do, though you've probably lost it anyway. It did get submerged in the river. I'd get a new film, if I were you, or a single-use camera. They probably sell them here.'

Elaine could tell from Marion's relaxed tone of voice that she had already assured herself that it wasn't the camera they were after, and that was probably what Rosalyn had dashed off to report.

'Yes, that's a good idea,' she agreed pleasantly. She hitched her rucksack on to her back.

She bought a single-use camera, another one, she reflected, ruefully, and they made their way back to the riverside. Only Grant and Pete were waiting for them.

'The rest have gone on ahead,' Grant announced. 'We thought it best to send someone to catch up with Kate and get a move on to confirm our bookings at Newcastle-on-Clun. Is that where you're staying?' he asked Elaine with seeming innocence.

'Yes.' As if they didn't already know. 'Is no-one's mobile working?' she asked with the same degree of innocence that Grant had used, knowing that Niall, at least, had one with him. She had purposely left hers at home, not wanting to carry the re-charger as extra weight.

'What? Oh, yes, I suppose so. It was mainly to tell Kate that you're all right. Are you ready for a stiff climb?' Adeptly changing the subject, Grant nodded upwards to Panpunton Hill. 'Niall was a bit concerned about you.'

'I'm fine,' she said lightly. 'Just lead the way.'

They zig-zagged their way to the top of the 400-foot climb and, now back on the dyke again, continued along it until they reached the summit ridge of Panpunton Hill.

They descended steeply but soon were climbing steeply up again through tall pine trees. Buzzards swooped and glided above them. It was breathtaking. They pushed ruthlessly onwards and could see that they were slowly catching up with the others.

For once, Elaine knew that she would be really glad the day was over. She felt worn and weary.

'Oh, we'll be last in line for the bath,' she groaned. 'It said in the guide book that it's a shared bathroom, and my bones know they've worked hard today.'

'Mine, too,' Marion agreed, though not with the same amount of feeling,

Elaine couldn't help thinking, reinforcing her conclusion that this group were not the run-of-the-mill non-walking group they had been made out to be. Where were their blisters, for heaven's sake? Not a blister between them.

Her thoughts led her into a cynical frame of mind. She couldn't help feeling as if Niall had already deserted her. Once he had been told she didn't have the much-wanted camera, he had high-tailed it after the others, having no longer any interest in her, it seemed.

She could see Niall away down the road. She recognised him by his fair hair and bright blue T-shirt. He was walking alongside Kate and seemed to be in conversation with her.

A sudden thought entered her mind. Now that the search of her rucksack had proved fruitless, he was pursuing the thought that Kate might have the camera.

She wished she were able to warn Kate to be less vigilant than they had been so far, to subtly leave her rucksack in an unattended place for a while. But, there was the added problem of Steve. She was sure Niall wouldn't try anything if Steve were around.

Niall and three of his group were waiting at the crossroads for Grant, Pete and Marion to tell them that Pete and Grant were to turn left and go to The Crown for the night.

'Book us in for dinner, Grant. How about you and Kate, Elaine? Should he book you in as well? Kate seems to think so.'

'Yes, that's fine,' Elaine agreed, speaking as lightly as she could. There was no point in trying to avoid being with the group.

'Good. We'll see you five later then.'

He nodded briefly at them and then fell into step between Elaine and Marion, turning to Marion and talking about the group's performance that day.

Since Elaine no longer believed their charade as a venture course, she listened with derision, trying to convince herself that she felt nothing for the man, that he was obviously up to no good and that it wasn't worth wasting any thoughts or sympathy upon him. She failed miserably.

She stole a sideways glance at him and her breath caught in her throat. He was so extraordinarily fit and bursting with magnetic charm. Feeling slightly weary, she dropped back half a pace and rested her eyes on him.

His charisma overwhelmed her natural reserve and she longed to be able to reach out and touch him, to feel once more the strength of his arms around her. Why did he make her feel like this? He was probably a criminal. Had she fallen in love with him?

She felt as though she had, but what did she know of him? Very little, if she were honest. But, what did one need to know to fall in love?

And what was the use? Once he had made sure that Kate didn't have the camera, he would leave, and she would never see him again, unless fate were kind enough to give them another chance . . .

Newcastle Hall loomed ahead of them. It was a large, double-fronted detached stone-built house, dating, probably, from the previous century. Patches of vines grew over its walls, partly covering some of the windows. The door stood open, awaiting their arrival.

Only Steve was in the entrance hall. He was crouched down over the rucksacks, fastening or unfastening one of them. He rose as they entered, re-awakening her suspicions about him.

'What are you doing?' she asked sharply, certain that it was Kate's rucksack he had been touching, not that it mattered. The camera wasn't there.

'Just putting away Kate's map,' he said mildly, 'like she asked me to. She's through there,' he added, nodding towards an open doorway. 'Mrs Reynolds said to take off your boots and join Kate in there, but leave your rucksacks out here. She hasn't quite finished the rooms yet.'

'Tea and coffee's ready, you guys!' Kate's voice sang out from the doorway. 'You all right, Elaine? I heard about your untimely dip in the river.'

Elaine grinned, suddenly recovering her good humour. She unhitched her rucksack and dumped it next to Kate's.

9

Later that evening, when they were once more on their own, Elaine brought Kate up to date over posting the maps home and then, after her untimely dip in the river, giving Rosalyn and Marion the opportunity to search through her rucksack.

'From your satisfied expression, I gather you had already got rid of the camera.' Kate grinned. 'What have you done with it?'

'Let's just say it's no longer in my possession,' Elaine told her.

At breakfast the following morning, Niall entered the dining-room with his mobile phone in his hand, his face serious.

'Something wrong, Niall?' Grant asked.

'Afraid so. It seems I'm wanted back at head office tomorrow morning. One of our international buyers has hit a problem.'

Elaine's heart lurched, even though she had been expecting Niall to be leaving soon. He had achieved his purpose in ascertaining that she didn't have the camera and was moving on.

'What shall the rest of us do?' Grant asked.

'Oh, I think you can continue without me,' Niall commented easily. 'I'll leave you in charge, Grant. You've been well-briefed with the route. You're making for Buttington today.'

Niall then let his glance swing over the whole table, carefully lingering no longer on Elaine than on any of the others.

'It's been great getting to know you all. I'm sorry to be leaving so abruptly but it can't be helped. You never know, our paths may cross again.'

'Are you leaving immediately?' Rosalyn asked.

'Yes. With it being Sunday, I've got to get back to civilisation as soon as I can and get to the nearest railway station that has a Sunday service, somewhere along the A49, that'll be. Mrs Reynolds is going to take me.'

Elaine knew that this was it then, the last time she would see him, and the others. She and Kate were only going as far as Montgomery today and meeting up with Val, a married ex-college friend, and her husband, Roy, who now lived on a farm near Newtown. They were spending the afternoon together and going to the farm for dinner, then back to Montgomery to sleep and be ready for an early start the next day.

They would be six or seven miles behind the group from then on, longer, if the group pressed on at a greater speed, if they continued with the walk. She wouldn't be surprised to learn that they miraculously disappeared from the scene.

Elaine deliberately took her time finishing her breakfast. She didn't want to give Niall the opportunity to speak to her on her own. It would be too much to bear.

As it happened, Steve also announced with regret that he was pushing on farther, not having the time off work, he said, to waste half a day's walking. Kate looked mildly mutinous and Elaine sensed her disappointment.

'We're booked in at Montgomery. We can't change it, because that would mean we would have to change the rest of our bookings,' Elaine reminded her.

They were both lost in their thoughts during the morning walk and it was with much relief that they arrived on the outskirts of Montgomery just before noon.

Here, they were met by Val and Roy, who had walked the couple of miles or so out of town to meet them. Their delight at renewing their friendship and having the opportunity to spend a few hours together lightened the mood and both girls outwardly overcame their despondency.

On Monday, the girls walked just

over eleven miles to Pool Quay, where they stayed in an antique dealer's house and on Tuesday, they set off once more, heading for a village called Trefonen, fourteen and a half miles away. It was a long walk through fields and farms, through dark woods and along river banks, made even longer by a heavy downpour of rain.

They were chilled and tired when they arrived at Rose Cottage and thinking only of whether they should have a hot bath or shower first, followed by a cup of tea, or whether to have the drink of tea first.

As it was, they settled for the latter, because Mrs Jones, their hostess for the night, met them with the news that a Mrs Harrison, their neighbour, had telephoned and wanted them to ring back as soon as they could.

Whilst Mrs Jones put the kettle on, Elaine made the phone call. Her heart raced. Was it to do with their parents?

'I'm sorry to disturb your holiday, love,' Mrs Harrison apologised, 'but I thought I'd better let you know that your house was broken into last night!'

'What is it?' Kate asked at her side. 'Are Mum and Dad all right?'

'Yes, it's not that. Our house has been burgled ... I'm sorry, Mrs Harrison. What was that?'

'I was saying that it doesn't look as though anything was taken. I think they must 'ave been disturbed. The cheeky beggars 'ad been rummaging through your post, I could tell that. I'd left it all nice an' neat on the dining-room table. Your mum and dad'll be upset when they hear. D'you think I should try and get in touch with them, too?'

'No. It would spoil their holiday and they wouldn't be able to do anything. We'd better come home and see to everything, though. I'll have to cancel the rest of our B&Bs. Will tomorrow be ... ?'

'Eh, no, love. Don't be doing that! There's nothing you can do, neither. We've already seen to getting the window fixed and our Tom's going to sleep in for you. You finish your holiday, love. You deserve it.'

'No, we must come back. It's not fair to you. There'll be the police to see to and everything.'

'Eh, love, the police have been and gone. They said the robbers were wearing gloves so there's no finger-prints nor nothing and no chance of catching 'em, neither! They said you can give 'em a list of anything that's missin' when you get home but, as I said, nothing seems to have been taken, unless you 'ad a thousand pounds hidden under your bed.' Mrs Harrison chuckled at the thought.

Elaine laughed with her, though it sounded hollow to her ears. She realised Mrs Harrison was talking again.

'I'm sorry, Mrs Harrison, I missed that.'

'Your friend? I was asking if she managed to catch up with you. She said she'd missed you at Chepstow and Monmouth and hoped to catch up with

156

you at Hay-On-Wye. I hope I did right letting her have the next few addresses and phone numbers so that she could book in with you.'

So, that was how he'd done it. The insight was like a lead weight settling in her stomach.

'Yes, Mrs Harrison, that's fine. Thank you.'

When Elaine had finally said goodbye and put the phone down, she repeated to Kate everything Mrs Harrison had said.

'So, what do you think, Kate? Should we go home or do as Mrs Harrison says and finish the walk?'

'We're due in Prestatyn on Sunday, aren't we? That's in five days' time.'

'Well, it's good company you'll be in, then,' Mrs Jones exclaimed. 'There's a Grand Carnival Procession in Prestatyn on Sunday! Something to do with United Nations, see, a World Peace Initiative, they're calling it. A series of peace talks are going on this week and then they're doing a whistle-stop tour of North Wales on Saturday and Sunday. We're off to Caernarfon on Saturday to wave our Welsh flags to them. Let them know we Welsh are behind them, we will. Anyway, come and get this cup of tea,' she invited, putting the local excitement to one side. 'That'll make you feel better.'

Elaine agreed, her mind dwelling more on what Mrs Jones had said about the peace talks. Surely that had nothing to do with the camera!

Or did it?

Was the Malaysian girl supposed to take a photograph of them? But, surely, any camera would serve the same purpose. There wasn't anything special about it. It wasn't even a good quality one.

She put the thought to Kate later, when she and Kate were on their own.

Kate looked sceptical.

'What's special about taking a photo of a load of foreigners? There'll be plenty in the local papers. I've been thinking more that someone had hidden a packet of drugs in it, you know, and given it to the Malaysian girl to bring into the country, and they want it back.'

'And burgled our house to get it.'

'Do you think that's what our house burglars were after? Did they get it, d'you think?'

Elaine pursed her lips.

'In answer to your first question, yes, I do. It has to be, doesn't it? But, no, he didn't get the camera.'

'He?'

Elaine shrugged despondently.

'Niall, I suppose. He's the only one who has our address. He mustn't have believed Rosalyn when she told him the size of the parcel. He thought I'd posted it with the maps.'

Kate's cheeks reddened slightly.

'And didn't you?'

'No. I posted it . . . somewhere else.'

They decided to do as their neighbour suggested and finish the walk. Elaine knew that if they went home, she would have to return to Prestatyn on

Sunday in order to see if the Malaysian girl did indeed try to contact them and try to get out of her what was behind it all.

Some of the enjoyment had gone out of the walk, though the girls did their best to appreciate the lovely countryside they were still passing through.

Their final full day's walk led them into the valley at Rhuallt. Elaine said nothing to Kate about the parcel she took back into her possession there. It was better that she didn't know anything about it.

They ordered an early breakfast for Sunday morning and managed to set off at eight o'clock, with a seven-mile last stretch to do.

'You'll be in plenty of time to see the carnival procession,' the receptionist said as they settled the bill. 'Quite a day it will be! Each nation is to have a decorated wagon and Miss World will be there to represent peace for the world. They're not due in town until about one o'clock.'

Elaine was beginning to feel very uneasy about it, much more so than before. What if it was something to do with one or more of the foreign delegates? And she was carrying a very-suspect camera.

It wasn't a hard walk that day, though parts of it were steep. The last few miles were spectacular, especially when they were high on the inland cliffs overlooking the town. From then on it was downhill and into the town teeming with people. It was a bit unnerving after the solitude of the past two weeks. She glanced at her watch. It was half-past seven.

'Let's go straight to the coast and walk into the sea,' Kate suggested. 'I . . . er . . . don't know if I told you but . . . er . . . I sort of arranged to meet up with Steve. He said he'd hang around until today, hoping we'd make it.'

'No, you didn't mention it,' Elaine replied. Oh, what was the harm? It was more or less certain that Niall had been the one after the camera. 'But, it's OK with me. I'll mooch around the information office. That's probably where the Malaysian girl will try to meet up with me if she's anywhere about. Our train leaves the railway station at four o'clock. Don't be late!'

They marched through the town, feeling a bit conspicuous with their rucksacks on their backs and heavy walking boots. It was a hot day and the hundreds of holidaymakers were dressed in summer clothes. Although there were still two hours to go before the carnival procession began, many hopeful sightseers were already claiming good vantage points.

Elaine and Kate walked out into the sea and Elaine asked a holidaymaker to take their photograph, using the last shot in the single-use camera she had bought.

After Kate had gone off to find Steve, Elaine decided to take her own camera to a chemist's shop, to see if it had dried out properly and, if so, buy a new film in case she had the opportunity to take a photo as the cavalcade passed by.

Elaine found a suitable chemist's shop.

'I fell in a river with it.' She laughed. 'I'm sure it's dried out but I just wondered if you would check it.'

The man took it off her and opened the back.

As he peered inside it, Elaine added, 'It doesn't really matter if it's ruined. I've had it for a few years. I didn't want to bring an expensive one with me.'

The man smiled and handed it back to her.

'It's perfectly dry,' he assured her, 'but you're wrong about it being an old one. This particular model only came out this year.'

Elaine stared at him. 'Are you sure?'

'Yes. It's got a small modification made to it that wasn't on the older ones. See, just here. The catch here was faulty on the older model. This one is quite secure.'

Elaine's brain was working overtime. This was the camera Steve had given to her, claiming to have retrieved it from the lad who had stolen it at Llanthony Abbey. Why had he given her a new camera? And, if it wasn't hers, how did he know her old one had been stolen? What was it to him?

The answer hit her between the eyes.

It had given him a reason to become acquainted with them, and in an admirable way. The restorer of stolen goods! He had said as much himself. He had lied! And if he had lied about that, he had more than likely lied about other things, like about the part Niall had played in costing him his job.

Not that Niall was innocent in all this. He was certainly involved in some way as well. But not on the same side as Steve.

But that didn't clear him, did it? He was up to something.

Elaine came to a sudden decision. She knew what she had to do.

'I'd like to buy another camera just like this. Do you have any for sale?'

It was quarter-past twelve when Elaine approached the Offa's Dyke Centre for the second time. Her eyes searched the crowds as she threaded her way, seeking the face of the Malaysian girl, hoping she would be able to recognise her. Would she be there? Would she come?

The fair hair of a man across the road made her breath catch in her throat. Although she couldn't see his face, she knew it was Niall.

He began to turn his head her way, slowly, carefully scanning the faces on Elaine's side of the road. It was Niall!

Although she had suspected that Niall wanted the camera for some reason, it hit her hard to see him there. She had held on to a faint hope that she was mistaken. Now, that hope had fled.

But she couldn't face him yet. Not until she had seen the Malaysian girl. He mustn't see her.

She ducked down a little and swiftly threaded through the crowds now thickly lining the pavements.

The possible enormity of what they had become involved in made her heart thump uncomfortably. What if things went wrong? She still didn't know what to expect, and they were running out of time.

She could see the information centre just ahead to her right. As she looked intently at the few people near to it, she felt a surge of relief. The Malaysian girl was there. She was anxiously scanning the crowds, no doubt looking for Elaine and hoping she would recognise her.

Elaine glanced around nervously. Nobody seemed to be giving her any attention. She unhooked the camera from around her neck and hurried forward.

'Hello!' she called.

The Malaysian girl turned towards her. Her smile of greeting faded abruptly as her gaze darted to Elaine's right.

Approaching her with his hand outstretched was Steve Martin. Behind him stood Kate, looking slightly bewildered, but Elaine's eyes didn't linger on her sister. Steve's voice pulled her attention back to him.

'Sorry, Elaine, but I'll take that!'

10

Niall scanned the faces of the crowds lining the opposite pavement. He and Grant had walked up and down this stretch of road all morning. Had something delayed them?

His breath suddenly caught in his throat. Was that Elaine? It had been just a brief glimpse of her hair. He concentrated his gaze but the face was gone.

This was nerve-wracking. Was Elaine part of it? He still couldn't be sure. She was mixed up in it somehow, he knew that.

He felt suffocated by the crowds. How could he hope to find Elaine, the Malaysian girl he'd seen in the café at Cardiff or Steve Martin in this throng? Where would they have arranged to meet?

As he stared around, he caught sight

of two young men across the road. They were dressed in hiking gear and were striding out purposefully towards the town centre. Where were they going?

He pushed his way to the front of the crowd. Traffic was being stopped now and mounted police were slowly advancing along the road, making sure that the barricades were still in place. Niall put his hand on top of the metal barrier. He lithely vaulted over it and darted across the road.

He quickly caught up with the two men and made himself relax his manner.

'Hi! You made it then!'

'Pardon?'

The men were surprised at his greeting.

Niall smiled.

'I think I saw you not far from Monmouth last week. You've been walking Offa's Dyke, haven't you?'

'Yes, that's right. Why do you ask?'

Niall grinned ruefully.

'I promised to meet my girlfriend at

the end of the walk about lunchtime today, but she didn't say exactly where. I didn't dream there'd be so many people about. She'll give me an earful if I'm late, I can tell you. Where do you think she might be?'

'Either at the Offa's Dyke Centre along the promenade, or standing in the sea having her photo taken,' one man suggested. 'Either place, it's that way.' He nodded towards the town centre. 'Just follow this road.'

He caught sight of Grant still on the opposite side of the road and made a large pointing gesture with his outstretched arm.

Niall set off as swiftly as he felt able to without drawing too much attention to himself. The uneasy feeling in his chest intensified. That must have been Elaine he had seen!

There she was! He could see her a few yards ahead. He opened his mouth to call her name but, as he did so, he saw a Malaysian girl step towards Elaine with a hesitant smile. She was the same girl he had been following in Chepstow Castle. Maybe he should wait until Elaine had handed the camera to her. That would connect the Malaysian girl to it as well as Elaine.

The girl's eyes slid to her left.

Niall followed them.

Kate was there, frozen into immobility, and Steve Martin! He was reaching out to take the camera, asking for it, it seemed.

He didn't want the camera in Steve's hands! It was too risky!

'Don't give it to him, Elaine!' he shouted sharply.

Elaine jumped and turned towards him. He could see the shock in her eyes. Her eyes wavered from him to Steve. They were equidistant apart, forming a triangle. The Malaysian girl was slightly behind Steve, looking uncertainly from one to the other. She was almost certainly a mere pawn in the game and could present no danger.

Steve's eyes glinted coldly as they recognised him.

'Stay out of this, Foster! Don't trust him, Elaine!'

He moved forward but Elaine backed away, eyeing them both with uncertainty.

'The camera is mine, Elaine,' Steve said softly. 'You know that! I gave you mine by mistake. Come on, hand it over. There's a good girl.'

'Don't believe him!' Niall said swiftly, realising that Elaine still didn't know which one of them to trust. 'Why are you doing this, Steve? Are you selling your country for the price of gold again?'

Elaine backed away again, almost melting into the backs of the people facing the road. Muttering complaints at her for bumping into them, the people nevertheless moved over a little.

'Not money, this time!' Steve responded, momentarily pausing. 'This time, it's principles. Peace talks! Huh! It's like Neville Chamberlain all over again with his 'Peace in our time.' The only way to peace is to get rid of the opposition first! This will give them the message right enough!'

Niall ignored him. He had heard it all before. His attention was on Elaine's face, seeing her emotions flicker uncertainly.

'You know I won't harm you, Elaine. I love you. Toss the camera to me. I'll catch it,' Niall called softly. He saw Elaine's eyes flicker with light but he didn't have time to dwell on the reason. A loud cheer began to rise farther along the road nearer to the town centre.

The sound increased as it rippled towards them and Niall realised that the carnival procession was slowly heading their way.

Niall saw Steve stretch his neck in the direction of the sound and then glance swiftly back towards Elaine. There was a calculating gleam in his eyes and Niall sensed that he had changed his tactics.

Steve straightened his body, drawing back a little. He seemed to be weighing up the distance between himself and Niall ... and Elaine ... and the leading decorated wagon.

Elaine seemed to be swallowed and dragged backwards by the crowd as they surged forward in a continuous wave against the metal barrier. She disappeared from Niall's range of vision.

Steve's hand slipped into his pocket and withdrew something metallic and shiny. For a fleeting moment, Niall feared it was a gun and that Steve was going to shoot, but that didn't make sense. He couldn't get near enough to shoot anyone in any of the cars now and he would have no chance of escape.

Even so, Niall felt himself reacting involuntarily.

'No . . . o . . . o!' he shouted as he dived forward towards Steve's legs, intending to bring him down to the ground before he could fire.

As he dived forward, Niall realised his mistake. It wasn't a gun in Steve's hand, but a mobile phone and even as their two bodies crashed to the ground, Steve's thumb was stabbing determinedly at the key-pad.

Niall suddenly knew! He was sending a radio-controlled signal to the camera. It was a bomb! It would blow up everyone and everything within a definitive radius.

Whilst his mind waited for the all-engulfing explosion to roar out, his body continued its desperate struggle to disarm Steve.

His attack had been aimed at Steve's legs, which left both of Steve's arms free. With his empty hand, he swung at Niall's head, knocking him back against the hard pavement, momentarily dazing him and then stabbed again at the keypad of the mobile phone in his other hand.

Niall hung on to his legs and took them both over into a roll. He managed to claw his way up Steve's body and landed a blow against Steve's head. Steve rolled his head with the blow, still trying to activate his phone.

Strong arms dragged the two men apart and hauled them to their feet. From the efficiency of their actions,

Niall sensed they were well-trained for the job and must be part of the police force or armed services. He gave up any resistance, knowing it would be futile to continue.

Steve's agitation and bewilderment that he had been unable to detonate the bomb gave him great satisfaction. Whatever had gone wrong, it was fortunate that it had done so, as he knew that his successful dive to bring Steve to the ground was too late to have prevented it!

A number of armoured steel vans had appeared from nowhere. Steve, arms handcuffed behind him was hustled into one and he, similarly restrained, was pushed into another. Niall knew better than to protest his innocence. A complete debriefing would be carried out in due time.

When the van stopped and the back door was flung open, Niall could see that they were in a cobbled yard, surrounded by high walls and high buildings. He staggered down the step, blinking in the bright sunlight. A few yards away, Steve Martin was entering the building under restraint and, just stepping out of another vehicle were Elaine, Kate and the Malaysian girl, under lighter restraint.

His debriefing didn't take long. He had the necessary code words and numbers to be checked and a few telephone calls from his superiors had soon made clear that he was a bona fide official appointed to the case and he was free to go.

'If you'll just step this way, sir,' a junior officer invited him. 'There's a young lady to see you.'

His heart leaped . . . and rightly so.

'Elaine!'

He strode across the room and gathered her in his arms. He drew back a little and held her from him so that he was able to look down at her face. She was smiling . . . that was a good sign!

'When I saw you dive at Steve, I felt sure he'd be desperate enough to kill you if he could, or you kill him! I still wasn't totally sure which one of you, if either, I could trust.'

'It was lucky for all of us that he didn't manage to blow up the camera. We'd all have been killed and possibly some of the international peace delegates as well.'

'Luck had nothing to do with it!' Elaine grinned triumphantly. 'I did what I should have done days ago. I bought another camera as a dummy and went to a police station with the real one and told them everything I knew. I think they thought I was a nutty female at first but my refusal to let them touch the camera until they promised to have it looked at by a safety expert made them take me seriously. They asked if I could help them set up the trap.'

'Which you did beautifully, my love. You were very brave.'

'I was very scared.'

'That makes you even more brave, and I love you even more for it.'

Her eyes softened but she drew away a little.

'Do you really love me? I feared I was just someone you used and dispensed with once I was no longer needed.' She paused for a moment and then spoke again. 'Tell me this, Niall. Did you have anything to do with the various burglaries that dogged our steps?'

'I have to confess to getting the lad to steal the camera at Llanthony, but he took the wrong one. And we made use of the break-in at Discoed. Rosalyn searched your things whilst the rest of us were outside. As you know, she didn't find anything, but I felt sure you still had the camera.'

'Why didn't you make a greater effort to get it back?'

'I decided that it didn't really matter, as long as we knew who was carrying it. We suspected Steve Martin, but had no proof. We wanted to witness the handover in order to trap more operatives. We still weren't sure what sort of weapon it contained, just that there were rumours of an assassination attempt on one or more of the foreign delegates at Prestatyn today. So, I quickly gathered together a group of colleagues and set out to trail you to Prestatyn, hoping you would lead us to the real villains of the piece. Once it was clear you no longer had the camera, I knew we had to look for other angles, but the trail still led to Steve Martin. I knew you must have posted the camera to somewhere nearby, your last B&B, I presume. So, I waited for you to arrive.'

He gathered both of her hands in his and drew them up to his lips, where he kissed the backs of her fingers, keeping his eyes on her face.

'I'm sorry I blew hot and cold with you. I got carried away in the pool at Hay-On-Wye and had to pull back to maintain my cover. 'But first . . . ' His face became serious again. 'I think we should sort a few things out. I'm a special investigator generally, working undercover on drugs or counter espionage. It's a dangerous job and I've got a few more years to serve before I'm due to take severance. There'll be times when I won't be able to tell you what I'm doing or where I'll be going. Can you bear to live with that?'

Elaine sobered immediately but it didn't take her long to consider.

'It would be harder to walk away from you and not be part of your life,' she admitted.

'Then we'll have to make sure that our time together is quality time, won't we? Starting from now!'

Niall lowered his head and his kiss said everything else that Elaine wanted to know.

Other titles in the
Linford Romance Library:

A HEART DIVIDED

Karen Abbott

During World War Two, the German occupation of Ile D'Oleron, off the west coast of France, brings fear and hardship to the islanders. As the underground freedom-fighters strive to liberate their beloved island, Florentine Devreux finds her heart torn between two brothers. But it seems she has fallen in love with the wrong one! The events following the Normandy landings force her to think again — but has her change of heart come too late?

SHADOW OF THE FLAME

Sheila Belshaw

When zoology student Lisa Ryding first meets wildlife film-maker Guy Barrington at Oxford University, she is prepared to follow him to the ends of the earth. But a secret too tragic for Guy to reveal makes this impossible. Five years later, they are thrown together on a remote game reserve in Zambia by their mutual passion to save the elephant from extinction. When Guy is bitten by a snake and nearly dies, Lisa realises that nothing will ever change her love for him and her only salvation will be to never see him again.

ECHOES OF YESTERDAY

Rachael Croft

Vet Keira Forrest thought she'd seen the last of GP Daniel Grant after he callously dumped her best friend, but now she finds herself having to give him emergency first aid after an accident. Worse, her new job is right next door to his surgery and the local matchmakers are busy. She is determined to avoid him, but an engaging wolfhound puppy named Finn and a family of delinquent cats have other ideas.

CLOUDED PARADISE

Rachel Ford

Luke Devinish was not the sort of man that one expected to find living on a quiet Caribbean beach, and he'd built his hut right in the middle of the land that Catherine wanted to sell! He made it very clear that he had no intention of moving, and an obscure law meant that Catherine couldn't evict him. However, she was eventually forced to admit that Luke and the sultry atmosphere of the Caribbean were an irresistible combination . . .